"...Amanda A. Bennington was a fighter, and she preferred to face her adversaries, not hide from them. She

RENEGADE TEXAN

Becky Barker

A KISMET™ Romance

METEOR PUBLISHING CORPORATION
Bensalem, Pennsylvania

KISMET™ is a trademark of Meteor Publishing Corporation

First Printing July 1991.

ISBN: 1-878702-49-1

Printed in the United States of America

To Mother and Daddy for a lifetime of love.

With special thanks to Roz Noonan.

BECKY BARKER

Becky Barker lives in rural Ohio with her husband, Buzz, and their three children: Rachel, Amanda, and Thad. Becky is a staff writer for a weekly newspaper and is an advisor for the central Ohio chapter of the Romance Writers of America. She has been an avid reader of romance since grade school and considers herself one of those lucky people whose life has been filled with music, laughter, and love.

PROLOGUE

Was it always this quiet? Tamara wondered as she spent another late night behind the desk in her office. Had the air conditioning always made such eerie noises? Had weird shadows always danced along the windows? Normally, nothing could distract her from work. Was she on the verge of a nervous breakdown?

The telephone at her right hand jangled suddenly and Tamara nearly jumped out of her cushioned seat. Her heart seemed to lodge in her throat and her pulse rate accelerated. Scolding herself for foolishness, she picked up the receiver.

"Hello."

"Hello, Tamara." It was Skip's familiar, suave voice and Tamara cringed inwardly. There was nothing for them to discuss.

"Hello, Skip."

"You're obviously working late," he commented. "Why don't you let me stop by and take you out for a quiet dinner?"

"Thanks, but I don't think that's a good idea," she replied. A lingering touch of guilt kept her frayed temper in check, even though he was making a real nuisance of himself. "We agreed that we shouldn't see each other socially."

"*You* came to that decision," he countered sullenly. "I want to spend time with you. Maybe then you'll realize what a mistake you've made by postponing the wedding."

Tamara had to give him credit for persistence. She'd called the wedding off and returned his ring, yet he refused to accept no for an answer. Handsome, charming, and independently wealthy, Skip Reardon had never learned the meaning of the word no. He assumed she'd eventually honor his wishes by marrying him. Repeatedly denying the fact hadn't gotten her anywhere.

"I have a lot of work to do, Skip," she responded in a dismissive tone. She knew his blue eyes would glitter with indignation and his lips would tighten in a petulant frown, but she was weary of their verbal skirmishes.

"Well, I certainly wouldn't want to come between you and your work," Skip drawled. "We know that your family and the family business are far more important than a mortal man. Forgive me if I resent being jilted in favor of the real loves of your life."

Tamara sighed deeply. She was tired of this argument. Her family and the Bennington Department Stores would always be important to her. She lived and breathed for little else.

"Goodbye, Skip," she said quietly and hung up the phone.

Depressed, she rested her head in both hands and then groaned in distress when the telephone rang again.

She considered ignoring it, but her family would worry if they couldn't reach her.

"Hello."

There was a short, static pause at the other end of the line and Tamara's nerves grew taut. Her stomach tightened as the rough, rasping voice of her anonymous caller crackled through the line.

"Working late? All alone, Ms. Executive?" the taunting, but well-disguised voice had a sinister tone that sent shivers down her spine. She'd had several mysterious calls lately. No specific threat was ever verbalized, yet the caller was intent on harassing her. She responded in a crisp, businesslike tone.

"Bennington Department Stores, Tamara Bennington speaking. May I help you?"

A grating laugh echoed in her ears, reminding her of Marlon Brando's imitation of a Sicilian godfather. "That's good. That's real good, Ms. Executive," the rasping voice derided. "Have a safe trip home tonight."

The sharp click of the receiver sent another shiver through Tamara. She was insane to listen to this maniac's veiled threats. She should have her phone tapped or let her answering machine take all her calls. She'd take care of it next week. Right now, she was going home. There was no hope of getting any work done tonight.

Grabbing her purse, she quickly turned off lights, locked the office, and strode to the elevator, telling herself that she had nothing to fear in her own building. The security was the best money could buy. The Benningtons could afford the best.

When the elevator came to an abrupt halt, Tamara caught her breath in alarm and then mentally berated herself. The elevator always stopped abruptly at the basement parking level. She was just a bundle of nerves this evening.

"Good evening, Ms. Tamara," the night watchman greeted as she stepped from the elevator. "Ready to call it a night?"

Tamara managed a warm smile for the security chief. Even if her fears were irrational, she couldn't help being relieved by his presence.

"I'm calling it a week," she declared with feeling. She rarely ended her work week on Thursday, but she needed this three-day weekend. "Tomorrow I'm helping Katie buy some new clothes and pack for her summer vacation. Then Saturday morning I'll take her out to the ranch."

"I know your Uncle Harold and Aunt Lucinda will be glad to see you," he responded, lightly grasping her arm to escort her to her car. It was a routine Uncle Harold insisted upon.

Tamara welcomed the routine and mentally commanded herself to relax. She asked the guard about his family and tried to pay attention to his response, but she couldn't quiet her nerves. The underground parking lot was oppressively hot. The humid air made the silk of her dress cling to dampening skin, increasing her discomfort. She couldn't remember ever feeling such an intense foreboding of disaster.

As she and the watchman stepped from the protection of the building, they were caught in the glare of oncoming headlights. Then everything happened so fast that she would never recall all the details. She would remember the blinding light, the screech of tires, her own terrified scream, and the guard's quick reaction that saved her life by mere inches.

ONE

Rane Masters sat low in the easy chair, his long, jean-clad legs crossed at the ankle. The fingers of both hands lightly balanced the thick glass of whiskey resting on his lean, flat stomach. He seemed relaxed, but his attention was riveted on the conversation of the room's other two occupants.

Lieutenant Carlile of the San Antonio police force paced the floor, his tread silenced by the thickness of the plush carpeting. Rane had worked with the tall, wiry man on several occasions, but never on an official basis.

Harold Bennington was Carlile's opposite. At seventy, he was a short, plump, financially secure man whose only concerns were the health and welfare of his family.

"I'm really worried about Tamara," Harold said with a heavy sigh. He sat quietly behind his antique desk and sipped his drink. His normally clear eyes were clouded with concern.

"Last night's incident scared her badly. I had a long talk with her and begged her to take a vacation, but she doesn't think that's the thing to do. She doesn't want to alarm Katie and her staff anymore than necessary."

Rane growled low in his throat, but didn't comment. His companions knew how he felt about the subject of Tamara's safety.

"I was in agreement until that car nearly ran her down," the lieutenant said. "The incident with the defective brakes and the menacing phone calls might not be related, but that driver last night didn't leave any doubt to his intentions."

Rane's expression grew more grim at Carlile's words. If they didn't find a way to protect Tamara, the next incident could be fatal. Her luck would eventually run out.

"I've offered her the use of one of our safe houses, but she adamantly refuses. Since she's not a federal witness, I can't force her to cooperate," Carlile reiterated his position. "I don't have the manpower to watch her around the clock. Right now, she's just an unofficial player in a very dangerous game."

"Last night should have made her an official player," said Rane.

"She escaped harm," Carlile retorted.

"So, she won't become an official concern of the police department until she's dead?" Rane snarled.

"Unfortunately, the safe house is the only protection I can offer," Carlile replied. He was concerned, too, but his options were limited.

"Tell me more about your niece, Mr. Bennington," he asked. His department had compiled information on Tamara's professional life and personal details that were publicly recorded, but he wanted a better understanding of the stubborn, independent woman in question.

A smile softened Harold's features as he reminisced a little. "My sister, Caroline, married a mountain man from West Virginia and disappeared from our lives thirty years ago. Lucinda and I couldn't have children; and we sadly accepted the fact that the Bennington name would die with me."

"Then, about nine years ago, I opened our door and found seventeen-year-old Tamara carrying her sister Katie. She was dirty, exhausted, and haggard, but she didn't have to prove her identity to me. She's as beautiful as her mother and I felt as though Caroline had walked back into my life."

Harold's voice grew gruff. "Caroline and her husband were dead, but before my only sibling died, she instructed Tamara to bring Katie to Texas. God only knows how a penniless teenager crossed the nation with a four year old in tow, but she made it; and Lucy and I welcomed them with open arms. Those girls have brought us more happiness than we'd ever dreamed possible."

"And now Tamara has full control of the family corporation?" Carlile wanted to know.

"Yes," Harold continued. "She took an immediate interest in the company. She studied tenaciously, started at the bottom, and relentlessly moved through the ranks to executive assistant. Last year I gladly resigned the presidency to her. This past year she's doubled our profits."

"Is it important that she maintain such a high profile?"

"It's not necessary, but one of the ways she's gained

success is by always being available to her staff and customers.''

Rane downed the contents of his glass. If Tamara didn't become invisible for a while, she was likely to be killed.

"We have to do something right now," he declared tersely.

Carlile nodded and eased his lanky frame into a chair. "I'm no help. If Tamara won't cooperate of her own free will, there's nothing I can do. She didn't actually witness the murder, even if Tralosa is convinced that she did."

Anthony Tralosa was the head of a crime family with a history of illegal activities in south Texas. He'd recently been arrested for murder. An associate of Tamara's had witnessed the murder and was living under the protection of federal agents.

Tamara had also been in the vicinity of the murder, although she hadn't seen anything. Unfortunately, the Tralosa family seemed to believe she was another witness, or at least a risk to their defense.

Rane suspected they were responsible for Tamara's recent brushes with death. He knew Tralosa was ruthless, yet he had no evidence against the man or anyone in his employ.

"My plan is the most foolproof," he told them grimly, straightening in his seat and setting his glass on the desk.

"Tamara won't take kindly to being abducted and held captive for a month," Harold felt compelled to remind his young friend. "Running and hiding won't appeal to her in the least."

"If the two of you are planning anything illegal, I'd

better not hear it." Carlile paused, then asked Harold, "Would she cooperate if you insisted?"

"I've tried reasoning with her," Harold admitted with a sigh. "She's incredibly loyal, but she's also self-reliant and strong-minded. I don't want to exploit her love by insisting she do as I ask."

"You may not have a choice. We can't protect her if she won't let us. If she doesn't want to spend the month before the trial in a safe house, her only other choice is to take an extended vacation. Preferably some-place where nobody knows her."

"She's probably saving her vacation time for a long honeymoon," Rane clipped, pouring himself another drink.

"No," Harold countered, studying Rane. "She broke her engagement with Skip and canceled wedding plans a couple weeks ago while you were out of town. We planned a public announcement, but the recent turn of events delayed it. I've been so preoccupied with Tamara's safety that I forgot to mention it."

Rane sank heavily into his seat and stared at Harold. "You forgot?" How had he forgotten something so significant? A scorned lover could be dangerous. "A jilted bridegroom with an inflated ego like Skip Reardon's is always a threat. Don't you think he might be the one trying to hurt or at least scare the hell out of Tamara?"

Harold shook his head. "I doubt it. I never liked the man, yet I don't think he'd harm Tamara. She said he was angry and they argued, but he didn't give her any real trouble."

Lieutenant Carlile didn't like it. "Never underestimate the power of vengeance. More crimes are committed in a passionate rage than in desire for monetary gain. It's possible we're barking up the wrong tree. This jilted fiancé might be our culprit.''

Rane spoke in a carefully guarded tone. "Until we know who's trying to hurt her, our major concern is her protection. We have to get her out of San Antonio until we can insure her safety.'' He turned brooding eyes on Harold. Although he was surprised that Tamara had called off the wedding, he was more alarmed at how deeply the news affected him.

"If you can help me get her on my plane, I can fly her out of Texas and out of harm's way. She'll resent our interference, but she'll know that we're acting in her best interest.''

Harold's expression tightened. "Tamara might cooperate if I insist, but not without one hell of an argument. She'll probably think I'm being bossy and over-protective.''

"Could you threaten her position with the family business or her private inheritance?'' Carlile wanted to know.

"That would hurt her, but it wouldn't deter her,'' Harold explained. "She's intelligent, ambitious, and hard working. Her success doesn't depend on family backing.''

"It couldn't hurt to remind her that you're responsible for the secure life-style she and her sister enjoy. You legally adopted them, so they carry the family name due to your generosity,'' Carlile declared.

Harold winced. Tamara owed him nothing. She and Katie gave far more than they received, yet Tamara had always insisted she owed him a debt she could never repay.

"I don't think talking will work at this point. I want to protect her,'' he conceded tiredly, "even if it means going against her wishes and using Rane's plan. She'll be furious for a while, but she has a forgiving nature. I'll just pray she understands my decision."

"In the meantime," Rane added, "I'll have some of my ranch staff guard the rest of the family. When Tamara disappears, the lowlife stalking her might turn his attention to her family."

There was a short silence as they considered a new concern. If anyone knew of Tamara's dedication to her family, they might try to get to her through her loved ones. If Tralosa was behind the attempts on her life, no one dear to her would be entirely safe.

"When will you put your plan into action?" Carlile asked, wanting to know the details.

"Tamara's bringing Katie here to the ranch in the morning. Now that school's out for the summer, Katie will be staying with Lucy and me. There are a lot of things on the ranch to keep a thirteen year old busy, and Tamara can come out most weekends."

"Could you be ready tomorrow?" Harold asked Rane.

"All I need to do is make a few phone calls," he said.

Carlile rose and shook hands with both men. "I'll trust you to take care of the matter," he said as he prepared to leave.

Harold's smile was grim, but determined. Rane didn't comment. The room was quiet until they heard Carlile close the front door behind him.

"You can count on me to keep Tamara safe," Rane swore. He had his own debt of gratitude to repay. Harold had befriended him when many of his Texas neighbors had deliberately ignored his existence. He was a trusted friend and Rane would do almost anything to help him.

The older man smiled warmly. He had no doubt that Rane would take care of Tamara, but Rane didn't realize what a strong-willed little tyrant his niece could be. She wasn't likely to obey orders without a fight and she might never forgive their high-handed belief that they knew what was best for her. Only time would tell.

Tamara Jo Bennington sighed deeply as she gazed at the panoramic view outside her bedroom window at the ranch. She'd helped Katie unpack and was looking forward to a weekend of relaxation, but she couldn't seem to relax.

This room at her uncle's had been a haven for the orphaned waif she'd been nine years ago. To a backwoods teenager, it had seemed like a fairy-tale castle and she'd felt like Cinderella.

Now, she just felt like a fool; a heavy-hearted, confused fool. She was supposed to have been a June bride, but she'd canceled the wedding. It hadn't been an easy decision to make, yet her feelings for Robert Avery Reardon III, Skip, had undergone dramatic changes these last few weeks. She couldn't ignore her doubts and fears any longer.

They'd decided early in their engagement that they'd wait until they were married before they slept together, but Skip had been pressuring her for more intimacy each time they were together. Tamara had found herself cringing when he became too passionate.

Skip had also agreed that Katie could live with them when they'd married. Despite Harold's and Lucinda's willingness to have Katie, Tamara never considered leaving her sister permanently in their care. Katie was her responsibility and she thought Skip understood how strongly she felt about the subject. Instead, he'd spent hours trying to convince her to send Katie to boarding school.

The last date she'd had with Skip had been very pleasant. He'd been especially charming. Tamara had begun to think they could work out their problems. Then he'd confessed to another change of heart. He'd decided he wanted children of his own.

Katie was the only family Tamara ever intended to have. She'd learned the hard way that raising a child was an awesome, sometimes terrifying experience. Skip had agreed that he didn't want children. But that was just another lie to seduce her into marrying him.

Tamara didn't know Skip at all. She nearly panicked when she realized how little she knew the real man behind the southern gentleman's facade. Accepting his proposal had been a mistake. She wanted to put it behind her and get on with her life.

Unfortunately, life hadn't been so smooth sailing lately. First, her brakes had failed. The car had been damaged, but Tamara had escaped injury. Then the crank phone calls had started—both at home and at work—making her a nervous wreck.

Thursday night someone had deliberately tried to run her down. She shuddered at the memory. It was the second brush with death she'd had in two weeks and she was afraid somebody *wanted* her injured or dead.

She couldn't ignore the facts anymore, or discount Harold's concerns for her safety. She'd told her uncle that she didn't want a bodyguard, but she'd reconsidered and would tell him so today. Perhaps Lieutenant Carlile could suggest a suitable person for the job.

Someone might believe she was a threat to Anthony

Tralosa, but she'd signed a police affidavit declaring she hadn't seen anything the night Tralosa allegedly killed a man. She and an associate had shared dinner; then gone in opposite directions. Carla had seen a murder, but Tamara was being threatened.

Could Skip be responsible? Surely not. He'd been irate when she'd broken their engagement and he refused to accept her decision as final, but he'd never been violent. It just didn't make sense. Nothing in her life made sense right now.

Tamara slipped out of her casual clothes and put on a royal-blue bikini she'd bought for her trousseau. She wasn't going to be using it in the Bahamas, but she could use it on the patio while sunbathing. Now that the wedding was off, she had some free time again. It had been months since she'd relaxed and today was Saturday. She didn't plan anything more stressful than smoothing on some tanning oil and lifting a glass to her lips.

"Tammy Jo?" Katie's voice proceeded her into Tamara's room. "Wow!" the younger girl exclaimed as she caught sight of the bikini barely covering her sister's lush body. "That's some suit. I hope you're not going to get it wet. If it shrinks, you'll be naked."

Tamara laughed. "Then I could just sunbathe in the nude," she teased wickedly. "I'd be sure to get an even tan."

"Just hope you don't get burned," Katie advised in exaggerated concern. "You'd have to stay naked for a week."

Tamara laughed harder and hugged her sister. "You are an incorrigible brat."

"Am not," Katie argued. Arguing was one of her favorite pasttimes. "I'm a pacifist."

"Well, where are you going, Ms. Pacifist? You didn't put on that fancy new sundress to sit on the patio with me."

"Aunt Lucinda asked me to go over to the Connors' for a visit. She and Sybil have some committee work to do." The Connors were neighbors of the Benningtons. They were nice people who just happened to have a teenage son Katie's age.

"I don't suppose Aaron is helping with this committee?"

"You don't think I'm going just to see him, do you?"

"No!" Tamara denied in a scandalized tone.

Katie changed the subject. "Do you think I'll ever look as good in a bikini as you do?"

Tamara rolled her eyes and put on the wrap-around skirt that matched her suit. Katie was only two inches shy of her sister's five-foot-six inches and Tamara knew she'd have the figure to fill a bikini before long.

"In another year, I'll have to worry about you borrowing my clothes. This is off-limits. It's not intended for public display."

"You sound like a prude, but you look like a centerfold."

"What do you know about centerfolds?" growled Tamara, propping her hands on her hips.

Katie put her hands on her hips and imitated her big sister's indignant stance.

Lucinda chose that moment to enter the room. She was several inches shorter than the other two. Her figure was round, her dark hair suspiciously free of gray, and her eyes bright with enthusiasm for life. She loved to tease and scold, but her heart was marshmallow soft.

"Well," she declared lightly, "it won't be long

before people are mistaking you two for twins." The sisters shared similar bone structure, the same wide, caramel-colored eyes, and thick, curly chestnut hair. "Then I suppose Aaron Connors will have to guess which one of you is just right for him."

"Aunt Lucy!" Katie complained while Tamara laughed happily.

"I know, I know," Lucinda apologized. "You are not romantically interested in Aaron Connors, you just admire his athletic abilities."

"That's right," Katie insisted. "He's going to teach me how to do some Olympic dives."

"Well, let's get going, then. I wouldn't want to destroy your chance to train with an Olympic star."

Katie gave Tamara a peck on the cheek.

"You're sure you don't want to go with us?" Lucinda asked Tamara as they headed toward the stairway.

"Absolutely, but say hello for me and have a good day."

Tamara was smiling as she turned to her dressing table and brushed her hair. She haphazardly fastened it on the top of her head with hairpins. The unruly curls were a nuisance unless she kept them tightly bound. She was usually more particular about neatness, but she didn't feel like messing with it today.

After slipping her feet into comfortable sandals, she left the room and headed downstairs, lifting the hem of her skirt to navigate the steps. As she walked, the side-split skirt revealed her slender legs.

Rane Masters was just entering the front door as Tamara descended the stairs. The sight of her made him catch his breath. He stood utterly still, enjoying an unexpected display of bared flesh.

The first thing that caught his eyes was a long, shapely leg exposed by the cut of her skirt. Her narrow waist was followed by the smooth skin of her stomach and rib cage. A scrap of shimmering blue fabric molded, but didn't disguise the firm, rounded fullness of her breasts. Her neck and throat looked so satin-soft that his mouth went dry with a sudden urge to plant kisses there.

Tamara was nearly at the bottom of the stairs before she noted his presence. The sight of him startled her, and she stumbled on the last step. Rane's big, warm hands grasped her waist to steady her. For a long moment neither of them seemed to breathe. Something in his gaze was totally unexpected and unnerving.

"You look lovely today," he told her gruffly, keeping a firm hold on her waist.

Lots of people had told her she was lovely, lots of times. But the smoldering look in his eyes and the thick, sexy tone of his voice made her feel special. She trembled in reaction to his husky compliment and her flesh burned where his hands touched it.

Harold chose that minute to enter the hall from the library, and Rane stepped aside so that Tamara could turn toward her uncle. Harold's eyes lit with pride as he moved toward them.

"Tamara, I'm so glad you decided to spend the weekend here!" he exclaimed, giving her a brief hug.

Tamara returned his hug and planted a kiss on his cheek. She knew he was concerned for her safety, but she hoped to alleviate some of his fears when they had a moment alone.

"I spent yesterday at the shopping mall with Katie, so I was in need of rest," she teased, not wanting to mention bigger problems in front of Rane. "Have she and Aunt Lucy gone already?"

"They just left," Harold replied, taking her arm and leading her toward the living room while motioning for Rane to follow. "Katie was in a hurry. Something about learning to dive."

Tamara grinned. "In that case, I'll leave you men to talk business. I'm going to find a lounge chair and do some serious lounging." Rane was a frequent guest. She made a habit of disappearing when their visits happened to coincide.

"Please don't rush off," Harold pleaded gently. "Sit down and relax. Let me get you a cold drink. What's your pleasure?"

"I'll just have a diet cola," Tamara agreed and sat down, feeling somewhat exposed. She draped the skirt modestly over her legs, but her breasts strained against the top. "These outfits aren't too practical. They're designed strictly for modeling."

"The designer was probably male," declared Rane, enjoying the view of silky-smooth flesh. His eyes were admiring as they met Tamara's and he grinned wickedly when her eyes flashed in annoyance.

Barbarian, she thought in irritation, feeling herself blush warmly. Masters was one of the few men in her acquaintance who made her acutely conscious of her femininity.

"Thank you," she told Harold as he handed her a frosty glass. He gave Rane a glass, then settled on the sofa beside Tamara, sipping his own drink. Tamara drank thirstily, trying to cool her heated reaction to Rane's marauding appraisal.

"What's on your agenda for the rest of the day, Tamara?" asked Harold.

"Not much, just a few hours of sunning myself by the pool."

"Nothing pressing today?" he queried.

"Nothing that can't wait," she replied, wondering why he was watching her so intently.

"Good, good," Harold declared in satisfaction, nodding his head in approval. "You should just take it easy and enjoy yourself for a change. You work too hard."

"How is the department store business?" Rane asked, his eyes also watchful.

"Everything is running smoothly, right now. I've been delegating a lot of the management decisions to my assistants, and they're doing a great job." She leaned back on the sofa, suddenly assaulted by drowsiness.

"It's always wise to have people working for you whom you can trust when you're unavailable," Harold said.

Tamara nodded, amazed at how heavy her head felt. Although she hadn't been sleeping well at night, she rarely got sleepy during the day.

Carefully leaning forward, she placed her empty glass on the coffee table. Then she lifted a hand to her mouth as a yawn escaped. "Excuse me," she begged their pardon as she yawned. "I must be more tired than I thought. I'd better go outside before I fall asleep. Then I can sunbathe and nap at the same time."

"Please don't go just yet," Harold begged. "I rarely get a chance to spend time with you these days. You're always so busy with the stores and you don't visit nearly often enough."

Tamara smothered another sudden yawn. "Pardon

me. I'm really sorry, I don't know what's come over me."

"You've been pushing yourself too hard," Rane replied. "You probably haven't been sleeping well and you need some rest."

"I guess you're right." Her voice slurred and Rane's image grew fuzzy. She started to rise from the sofa, but dizziness overwhelmed her, and she swayed unsteadily.

Rane's strong arms were ready to scoop her off her feet. Tamara's eyelashes fluttered as she drifted to sleep.

"What did you give her?" he asked Harold.

"It's a fairly mild, but fast-acting sedative," the older man assured. "It won't harm her, but it will keep her quiet until you have her aboard your plane. Is everything ready?"

"So far, so good," replied Rane roughly, his eyes intent on the delicate beauty of Tamara's face. He was a little shocked by the sheer delight of having her in his arms.

Harold led the way from the house and helped Rane tuck Tamara into the backseat of his Mercedes. "I had one of my ranch hands take her luggage to the airfield," he said. "But I haven't given the details of our plan to anyone."

"Andrews is the only one of my men who will know exactly where we are," Rane reminded. "He can be trusted and you can reach us anytime through him."

"You have the letter I wrote Tamara?" With Rane's nod, Harold continued, "You can give it to her if you think you need some extra persuasion," he told the younger man.

"Do you think she'll cooperate?" Rane asked as he slid beneath the wheel.

"I hope so."

"We're doing what's best," Rane reiterated.

"I hope so. I sincerely hope so," Harold muttered as the car's powerful engine roared to life. "Godspeed."

TWO

Rane checked the instrument panel and eased his jet into a northwesterly flight path. He radioed their location to the nearest air-traffic tower and was granted permission to cross the Texas/Oklahoma border. The plan was progressing smoothly, yet he couldn't relax. He had no idea how Tamara would react when she woke, but he was mentally preparing himself for her wrath.

A special mirror allowed him a partial view of the cabin quarters and he could tell she was still sleeping soundly. He couldn't seem to stop looking at her. He'd found her intriguing since the first time they'd met and he felt inexplicably protective of her. He'd known a lot of women in his thirty-five years, yet none of them had affected him as Tamara did. Being introduced to such quixotic emotions at this stage of his life wasn't a pleasant or welcomed development.

The chemistry between them was explosive. Tamara determinedly ignored it, but he couldn't. When she'd collapsed in his arms earlier, his senses had reeled. Her soft, thick hair smelled honeysuckle-sweet and felt like raw silk against his skin. His pulse had surged when she'd snuggled close and tucked her head into the curve of his shoulder. He was happy to steal her from the constant threat of danger.

His next glance in the mirror caught a movement. She was still wearing her bathing suit, but he'd covered her with a light blanket. She lifted a hand and ran it through her hair. Rane wondered if she'd wake up as suddenly as she'd gone to sleep.

Tamara felt the trembling of powerful engines beneath her. Where in the world was she? The thought brought her eyes open. Lying flat on her back, she faced what looked very much like the ceiling of a plane.

Her head still felt heavy. She moved it cautiously, but there was no pain, just some lingering grogginess. Her hair was tumbling over her forehead and she shoved it aside with one hand. Then she took a more encompassing look around her.

She was safely strapped to a plush sofa in the luxurious cabin of a small jet. The realization caused immediate alarm. She searched for the clasp of the seat belt while she tried to remember what had happened. Was she being kidnapped?

Glancing down, she realized she was still scantily dressed. All she recalled was sitting in her uncle's living room drinking a cola.

Had she been drugged? Impossible. Not in her uncle's home! Then why had she gone out like a light? Did Rane Masters have something to do with this? Had he drugged her? No. Her uncle had given her the drink. Masters had merely scooped her in his arms when she'd gone weak. She trembled at the memory of those strong arms. She didn't want to think about the way that man affected her.

Unfastening her seat belt, she slowly rose to a sitting position and studied her surroundings. There was a small table and a couple of chairs. The other side of the cabin held an easy chair, a bar, and a desk. The furnishings were handsome, yet functional.

When she looked forward to the cockpit, she saw the form of one very large man. Then she met the pilot's eyes in the mirror. Masters. No one else she knew had eyes quite so dark and penetrating. What the hell was going on here?

Rising from the sofa, she was surprised at her initial weakness. How long had she been sleeping? What had made her sleep like the dead? At least her hands and feet hadn't been bound. Of course, there was little opportunity for escape from several thousand feet in the air.

She winced and squinted her eyes as she entered the sky-bright cockpit. Then she slid into the vacant copilot's seat and turned cold, demanding eyes on Masters.

"Tamara." He greeted her with a polite nod of welcome.

Her eyes flared at his audacity. "I want an explanation and I want it right now."

Rane briefly surveyed her sleepy, tousled beauty, then returned his gaze to the clear blue skies. "We're leaving Texas for a little while."

"Just like that?" she exclaimed when he didn't elaborate. "We're leaving Texas. No 'what do you think, Tamara?' No 'would you like to go for a ride, Tamara?' Just knock me out and strap me into your jet!" she raged in disbelief, her hands balled into fists.

Rane fought to contain a grin. Her angry sarcasm

lightened the weight of guilt he was feeling, although she wouldn't appreciate his reaction to her temper. She wouldn't understand his delight that she was furious, not frightened.

"You weren't knocked out," he finally replied.

"What did happen to me?" she demanded.

"Your Uncle Harold gave you a sedative."

That information diluted Tamara's anger with confusion. Her tone was troubled. "Uncle Harold drugged me? Why? Why would he do a thing like that? I'd do almost anything for the man, so why would he want me unconscious?"

Rane wondered if she really would do anything Harold asked. They were about to find out.

"Harold is worried sick about you. Especially after the recent attempts on your life. He tried to convince you to leave the city, but you wouldn't agree. So he decided to insure your safety by having me fly you out of state for a while."

Tamara was really confused now. How did she know that Rane Masters wasn't responsible for the threats on her life? Because he had no reason, her logical mind supplied. She might not like the man, but she knew Uncle Harold trusted him and Harold was an excellent judge of character. Besides, Masters hadn't given her the drink.

"Harold knows I can't just disappear. I have a business to run and people who depend on me. There will be problems to solve. And my friends will demand to know where I am."

"Harold is going to take care of the business. He ran Bennington's for years. With the help of your assistants, he can manage for a little while. You were due for a vacation, anyway."

It was true. Tamara had prepared her staff for a month-long absence while she was on her honeymoon. She knew they could handle the business, but she'd just finished explaining that she had canceled the wedding and that she didn't intend to take time off work. Her disappearance was bound to cause confusion.

She felt dizzy again. Her head was reeling with chaotic thoughts. She turned to study Rane. Even though she'd frequently seen him at her uncle's ranch, she'd always suppressed any desire to know more about him.

He was a big man, six-feet tall, and probably two-hundred pounds. Most of his body had the lean look of muscles; she didn't think he had an ounce of fat. He wasn't a bit handsome, yet his harsh features weren't unattractive. His hair was coal black, thick, and rather long. His skin was darkly bronzed. Harold had once mentioned that Rane was of American Indian heritage and his rugged profile supported that claim.

"Where are we?"

Rane tensed, but kept his eyes on the cloudless sky. The situation was about to get more difficult. "We're flying across the Texas border right now."

"Then you can just turn this thing around and fly back over the border," Tamara insisted indignantly. "I'll go home and discuss this with my uncle in a rational fashion without all the dramatics. I have no intention of taking a vacation right now."

"I'm afraid you don't have a choice," Rane told her.

Tamara didn't like his tone or the rigid set of his jaw. "Perhaps you'd better explain," she declared coolly.

"It's very simple. Someone wants you dead, and your uncle wants to keep you alive. If you're not anywhere to be found, then no harm can come to you. All you have to do is relax and let me worry about you for the next few weeks.''

"Weeks?" Tamara nearly exploded. "Are you crazy? I'm not going to relax. I'm certainly not going to let someone scare me away from work and my family. And I'm not staying with you for a day, let alone weeks!''

"Harold tried to convince you to hire a full-time bodyguard, yet you refused. He wanted you to take a vacation or go to a safe house until Anthony Tralosa's trial was over, but you wouldn't agree. He didn't feel as if he had any other viable choices. He loves you and wants to keep you safe.''

"I don't even know that Tralosa is behind all this trouble," Tamara argued. "And if I just disappear, I might never be sure. I was considering a bodyguard, but I didn't have a chance to tell Uncle Harold.''

In all the years she'd known him, Harold had never tried to control her. He'd offered advice and been supportive when she needed help, but he'd never tried to manipulate. Tamara realized that only desperation would prompt him to interfere now, especially in such a shocking manner.

She'd have agreed to almost anything he asked if she'd known he was this worried. She owed him and he was family. Still, she wanted a chance to discuss the matter thoroughly.

She'd let Masters deliver her to the chosen vacation spot and then she'd get in touch with Harold immediately. She didn't want to disregard his concern, but she had to make him understand her position. She couldn't just run away from the confusion in her life. She was used to solving her own problems.

Tamara Jo Bennington was a fighter and she preferred to face her adversaries, not hide from them. She would agree to a bodyguard and curtail her socializing until the authorities discovered who was trying to harm her. But she wouldn't hide.

Rane wished he knew what was going on inside her head. He was surprised at how calmly she was accepting Harold's authority. He'd heard that Tamara was one cool lady, always in control, but he'd mentally prepared himself for everything from temper tantrums to hysterics. Her calm was disconcerting. Was she incapable of displaying real emotion? Was her somewhat ruthless business persona the real Tamara Bennington?

"What's in this for you?" she asked him, as though the question had just occurred to her.

"Revenge. I believe Tralosa wants you dead and I have an old score to settle with him."

Tamara digested that bit of information and prodded for more. "What kind of revenge? What did Tralosa ever do to you?"

"You might say I was one of his very first victims and I want to see him go to prison for his crimes."

"The authorities have a strong case against him and I'm not involved," Tamara countered.

"He's a nefarious criminal, brilliant at protecting himself. I don't want anything disrupting his trial."

"But I'm no threat to him!" Tamara insisted for the hundredth time. "I didn't see him commit a crime."

"He obviously doesn't believe that and regardless of what he thinks, I promised Harold I would keep you safe."

"But your real objective is revenge," Tamara insisted.

Rane's head snapped around and his eyes locked with hers. He didn't like her tone, but he couldn't deny the facts. "It will be sweet revenge," he growled softly.

"What kind of grudge could justify the risk of a

kidnapping charge?'' she demanded. Wanting his full attention, she reached out and tugged on his shirt sleeve. "What did Tralosa do to you? Did he steal some land or cheat you out of money?"

Rane felt a swift, hot jolt of sensation where her hand touched him and his expression tightened. He hadn't intended to tell her the whole story, but her challenge wounded his ego.

"Because of Tralosa's greed, I spent time in prison. I was just a teenager and Tralosa was just getting started in his life of crime, but I paid the price while he's dodged the law all these years. He's long overdue for his own jail term."

She shifted her eyes back to the sky. Rane had spent time in prison. She didn't much like Harold's choice of companions. Was she being saved from a homicidal maniac by another hardened criminal? Better the devil you know? The problem was, she didn't really know Rane Masters.

At this point, there was little she could do to escape Masters. If nothing else, Harold trusted him, and they had devised a detailed plan for her protection.

Rane let Tamara mull over the situation as he radioed for permission to enter Arkansas airspace. Permission granted, he calculated at least another two hours to their destination.

"If you'd like something to eat or drink, there's a well-stocked bar and refrigerator in the cabin. Your luggage is in the closet if you want to change clothes. You might as well take advantage of the luxurious accommodations while they're available." Rane kept his eyes forward, but he heard her start of surprise.

He sounded eager to be rid of her, but Tamara was just as eager to leave the cockpit and see what clothing had been packed for her. Besides, she needed time to make her own plans.

Rane had an incredible urge to reach out and touch a silken thigh as she brushed close by him. He tightened his grip on the controls and forced himself to resist. The next few weeks would be fraught with temptation.

Tamara reentered the cabin of the jet and headed for the large, walk-in closet. She found her own luggage and quickly sifted through the contents. She found jeans, sweatshirts, and a few pairs of shorts. Where were they going? Surely not to any sunny resort area. The only lightweight clothing packed in her bags were sexy undergarments and scandalously flimsy negligees she'd originally bought for her trousseau.

Grabbing a pair of jeans, a lavender sweatshirt, and some comfortable running shoes, Tamara headed for the bathroom and changed. She felt less vulnerable in the practical clothing.

She quickly washed her face and brushed her hair. Whomever had done her packing had remembered most of her toilet items, but hadn't included any barrettes to confine her hair. She'd lost half of her pins, so had no choice but to leave it loose, even though she felt less confidant with her hair unrestrained and tumbling to her shoulders.

Tamara looked through her belongings once again, searching for her purse. She didn't know their destination, but she would need some identification and money or credit cards if she had to get home without Masters' assistance. She moaned when she couldn't find anything, yet she wasn't surprised. Harold probably hadn't thought she'd need her purse or briefcase.

Her next course of action was to raid the refrigerator. She was hungry and it would be wise to keep up her strength. Escaping Rane Masters would undoubtedly require an enormous amount of energy. It all depended on their destination and the outcome of her phone call to Harold.

After a snack of cold chicken, cheese, and fruit, Tamara sat on the sofa and drank a glass of cola. She was still feeling drowsy. This time, she knew she hadn't been drugged, but she assumed her body was still fighting the effects of the first sedative. Maybe it would be wise to rest a while. But first, she wanted to find out how much longer they would be in the air.

Rane tightened his grip on the controls as she rejoined him. The last thing he needed was emotional complications, yet he couldn't seem to remain indifferent to her. He wished she weren't so damned beautiful and alluring. He would have to curtail his increasing fascination with his lovely captive.

Tamara slid into the copilot's seat, her attention directed at Rane. "Where are we going?" she asked as calmly as she could manage. When she noted his tight expression and clenched jaw, she became wary.

"To a vacation place I own," Rane told her.

"Where?" Her tone hardened when she realized he didn't want to tell her the whole truth. She could feel his heightened tension and she didn't like it.

"The destination doesn't matter," Rane hedged smoothly. "You'll be safe there. Nobody can find you."

"For how long?" Tamara demanded tersely. "How long have you macho males decided to keep me hidden for my own protection?"

"You were planning a month's honeymoon," he reminded her quietly. "Tralosa's trial should be over in a month. Once he's convicted, you'll be safe again."

Tamara began to tremble violently. She was furious and felt helpless. After years of having her life under firm control, her secure little world was crumbling about her. She was both angry and frightened. Masters was a virtual stranger and she was temporarily at his mercy. She couldn't fly this plane and she had absolutely no chance of overpowering him in a physical confrontation.

"I can't believe my uncle would condone such an injustice. He would never agree to holding me against my will for an indefinite period of time!"

"Your uncle understands the situation and hopes you'll understand his motives. He'd do anything to protect you."

"With or without my consent?" Tamara snapped in her agitation. She grabbed Rane's forearm. "This is against the law!" she reminded him forcefully. "If you take me anywhere against my will, it's kidnapping. That makes you just as much a criminal as Tralosa. I want to go home and I want to go there now!"

The muscles beneath her grasp flexed powerfully. Rane's features were granite-hard and his eyes glowed with unnerving intensity. Tamara released his arm as though burned. She knew she was pleading a hopeless case, but she had to try.

"Let's compromise," she suggested. "If you take me home, I'll hire a bodyguard. That should appease Uncle Harold."

"I'm afraid there's not room for compromise," he told her firmly. "Your life has been at risk for weeks and you chose to ignore the warnings."

"I'll make up for it," she declared desperately. "I'll surround myself with guards and wear a bullet-proof vest!'' She hated to beg, but the circumstances warranted drastic measures.

Rane didn't respond, but his unbending manner was answer enough for Tamara. She commanded herself to stay calm. Arguing with him only made her more furious. She'd try reasoning with him.

"You can't possibly want to waste your time babysitting me. I know you have a ranch to run, and Uncle Harold said you still oversee the operations of your airline."

He was officially retired from his air-transport lines, but Tamara doubted if a man like Rane ever fully relinquished the reins of his business.

"Surely nothing Tralosa did twenty years ago could warrant a self-imposed exile from your life in San Antonio."

"The crime justifies the desire for revenge, and I'm just one of Tralosa's many victims," he ground out, temporarily ignoring her while he radioed the nearest air-traffic tower.

Tamara was curious about his involvement with the criminal world. "How did you get involved with Tralosa?"

Rane hadn't intended to give her details, but he decided to let her know how determined he was to see Tralosa punished.

He kept his eyes on the sky and his hands firmly locked on the controls. "I told you he was responsible for getting me imprisoned. My father and I were just launching the air-transport business, and Tralosa hired me to fly some cargo to Mexico. What I didn't know was that he managed to load contraband on the plane for the return flight. When I started to take off, the plane was surrounded by policemen. I was arrested, found guilty in a mockery of a trial, and incarcerated."

Incarcerated in a Mexican prison? The full extent of such a plight hadn't dawned on Tamara when he'd mentioned it earlier. Now she recalled all the horror stories she'd heard about Americans jailed in foreign prisons.

"If you were innocent, why weren't you cleared of wrongdoing and released?"

Rane gave her a look that hinted at her naiveté. "Our firm was struggling financially. There wasn't money for the big bribes the officials were accustomed to, but my plane was worth a considerable amount of money. By finding me guilty, they were entitled to confiscate my property."

Tamara's expression revealed her shock and outrage at such an injustice. "How long were you in prison?"

"Two years," Rane's reply was curt. He'd already told her more than he'd intended. He didn't want sympathy.

"How old were you when you were released?"

"Twenty-one going on one hundred," he answered. "You age fast in prison. I was released more than fourteen years ago, but the desire to see Tralosa punished is still strong."

Although Rane's incarceration, indignity, and humiliation had passed, he would never forgive Tralosa for the damage done to his family. "My father went bankrupt and died of a heart attack while trying to free me from prison. He'd never trusted Tralosa. Dad begged me not to accept a commission from the man, but I was young and headstrong and certain I knew what was best for the business."

Rane shook his head, still pained by the memories.

"My mother finally negotiated my release after my father's death." His mother had suffered an even greater injustice, but he didn't discuss that with anyone.

"Have you ever confronted Tralosa?"

"No. I didn't want to go back to prison for murder," Rane explained in a deadly tone that sent a shiver over Tamara.

"Since he established his little empire in southwest Texas, I've heard plenty about his disrespect for the law, but he's wisely stayed clear of me."

Tamara was overwhelmed by a sudden wave of exhaustion. His story had weakened her resolve somehow. She didn't have the strength to deal with more confusing emotions right now.

"How much longer?" She decided she needed some sleep and she couldn't bear to spend any more time in the cockpit.

"A couple of hours."

"Then I'm going to take a nap."

"Make sure you fasten your safety belt," was all Rane said.

Tamara did as he instructed. Once prone and secured, she tried to forget their conversation and concentrate on an escape plan. Skydiving from the jet wasn't a feasible option. Pitting her strength against this giant of a man wasn't a smart idea either. For the moment, she would rest. When they landed, she would have to stay alert, try to note their location, and await an opportunity to use her God-given talent for self-preservation.

It wouldn't be the first time she'd been forced to use those survival talents, she reminded herself grimly. She'd sworn to never be vulnerable enough to need such abilities, but she couldn't have known what a curve life would throw her.

It had taken nine long, hard years to rebuild her life and overcome her insecurities after her parents' deaths, but she'd survived. She thought she had already faced the worst fate life could bestow on her, yet now she wasn't so sure.

She drifted to sleep, content in the knowledge that she was a survivor. She could contend with nearly any obstacle thrown in her path. Rane Masters was the only unknown element she might have trouble handling.

THREE

When Rane entered the cabin after landing the plane, he found Tamara sound asleep. Pleased that she was resting, he quietly collected their luggage.

He decided to let her sleep while he greeted an airfield employee who helped him shift his and Tamara's belongings to a waiting helicopter. The last leg of their journey couldn't be made by plane.

Tamara still hadn't awakened when he was ready to depart, so he nudged her gently, but she was sleeping too deeply. She probably hadn't gotten the sedative completely out of her system, he thought, leaning down to lift her into his arms.

The instant he touched her, he was engulfed by the sweetness of her scent. He was tempted to bury his face in the silk of her hair as his arms encircled her. The firmness of her breasts pressed against his chest, and he moaned derisively. It was his own fault he was suffering this torture. He'd wanted time alone with her.

When her body curled trustingly against his, he knew

the torture had only begun. His grip tightened as her warmth permeated his entire being. He commanded himself to move without further delay. They only had another half-hour of flying, and he was impatient to reach their destination.

Tamara tried to drag herself to consciousness as she was being strapped into the helicopter. She gave Rane a confused look, but continued to doze despite the deafening noise of their aircraft.

She didn't come fully awake until the helicopter touched down. She knew without being told that they'd arrived at the location where Rane intended to "vacation" for the next month.

Darkness seemed to have enveloped them, and Tamara wondered if she'd slept away the entire afternoon. Then she realized they'd landed on a small helicopter pad amidst a cluster of tall pine trees.

She was aware of her captor unfastening her safety belt and climbing from the helicopter, but for the first time all day, she didn't care what he was doing or where he was going.

Her senses became highly attuned to their surroundings and an all-encompassing panic wove its treacherous way throughout her body.

She smelled the trees, felt the dampness of the foliage and could name the individual plants that made up the overall smell of the area where they'd landed. It was a nightmare, she told herself. She was still asleep and the old nightmares had returned to haunt her. The events of the day had stolen her self-confidence and threatened her control. Her mind was playing tricks on her.

They couldn't be in the mountains. She couldn't be on top of a mountain, any mountain; it was a fate worse than death and far more feared. Tamara pinched her arm to convince herself that she was caught up in some dreaded nightmare of the past.

There were goose bumps on her arms and she felt the pinching sting of her fingers. She was awake and more frightened than she'd been in nine years. She'd put this behind her once, and she didn't know if she had the strength to fight all the old pain and insecurity.

She couldn't fight the mountains, she declared in a silent scream of horror. Surely, no one would deliberately force her to fight the mountains!

Rane opened the door of the helicopter and stepped up to give Tamara a hand. When he lifted arms to assist her, he was caught off guard by the genuine terror in her eyes. His heart rate accelerated in an instant of inexplicable, wrenching emotion.

"Tamara?" What had caused her sudden fear of him?

Tamara couldn't respond. She was looking at him as though he were a reincarnation of the devil. She couldn't imagine anyone being so cruel as to bring her to this place, but she felt a deep, panicky fear of such a person.

"How could you?" she managed to ask in a hoarse whisper.

How could anyone know of her past? She was sure there was no earthly way to trace her life before she'd appeared on Harold's doorstep. Harold, Lucinda, and Katie didn't even know about the dark secret of her life before she'd gone to Texas. Masters might be capable of accomplishing what others considered impossible, but even he couldn't have done this without some unearthly sort of power.

"How did you know?" she repeated in a stunned tone as Rane lifted her easily to the ground.

He had an urge to clutch her close and demand an explanation, but he was wary of the incontrovertible fear in her eyes. What had frightened her so suddenly and so thoroughly?

"How did I know what?" he asked softly, coaxingly.

"Where are we?" countered Tamara, still wearing an expression of fear and confusion. "What mountains are we in?"

Rane couldn't tell her without jeopardizing his control of the situation and he wasn't ready to trust her that far.

"Does it matter so much?"

No. The name didn't matter. It was still a mountain and still a place to be feared above all others. Tamara wasn't sure if her kidnapper was being deliberately cruel or if he really had no knowledge of her background. But for whatever reason, the fates were relentlessly wreaking vengeance on her.

"Where are we going?" she asked with a lingering touch of panic. She fought to control her initial shock and fear, but she remained dazed by the frightening turn of events.

"I have a little cabin a few hundred yards from here," Rane replied, watching Tamara intently as she moved in zombie fashion. Was she suffering a delayed reaction to recent dangers?

"Are you all right?"

When Tamara made no response, Rane gently urged her to follow him as he led her down the path toward his log cabin. It suddenly occurred to him that she might fear being isolated with him. Perhaps she was afraid to trust him.

Whatever the cause, he was convinced that her fears were real and he was alarmed at how her emotions affected him. He'd never expected her to look at him with awe or delight, but he was deeply disturbed by the terror she'd displayed.

As they made their way down a small incline toward a plateau of level ground, Tamara's nerves were so highly sensitized by their surroundings that she suffered physical pain. A sweat broke over her body and the dampness of the air chilled her to the bone. She knew it was only late afternoon, but the thick foliage and heavily-wooded area didn't allow much sun to filter through.

Cold and darkness quickly weighed on her mind as well as her body. She was physically capable of surviving the elements, but could she survive the emotional trauma of finding her way off another mountain?

A fairly smooth path had been cleared through the rough terrain so that their trek wasn't hindered by much of the dense foliage. Rane preceded Tamara for most of the way, but when they reached more level ground, he turned to take hold of her arm and guide her the last few yards to the cabin nestled in a natural curve of the mountainside. He was alarmed by her stiffness.

A close scrutiny of her features alarmed him even more. Was she suffering from shock? He wanted to get her inside the cabin and make her lie down for a while. He was sure she'd regain her perspective once she realized he had no intention of hurting her.

"You're chilled." He tried to break the unnerving silence. "You'll feel better when you've had time to relax."

Rane reached for a key that was hidden over a window frame, then opened the door wide, turning to assist

Tamara through the doorway: but she wasn't budging. She was staring at the cabin as if it were the doorway to hell.

Afraid she was going to collapse, Rane scooped her into his arms. "You don't have to go shy on me. I'm not a spider inviting you into my parlor."

Tamara didn't respond. When he stepped over the threshold of the cabin, she stiffened and threw her arms and legs out to brace herself against the outer frame of the door. She made it clear that she didn't intend to be cajoled into entering his mountain abode.

Caught off guard by her strong, swift actions, Rane nearly dropped her. He tightened his hold and tried to move through the door at a different angle, forcing her to release her grip on the frame.

Tamara fought him each time he loosened her grip and attempted another move inside the door. As soon as he'd pry her fingers from one handhold, she'd grasp another portion of the woodwork with equal strength and determination.

Rane emitted a rough sigh and glared at her. He was getting nowhere and Tamara's resistance didn't seem to weaken.

"Will you be reasonable and stop fighting me before you get hurt?" he growled roughly. "I'm not going to attack you the minute we step through the door, so you can stop behaving as though your life is in peril."

He knew that his words didn't make any impression on her. Her features were frozen and she looked at him with a grim determination that he couldn't understand.

"You'll feel better once you're inside and can rest," he said, trying to reason with her.

"No," was her clipped response as she tightened her hold on the outside wall of the doorway.

The next time Rane pried her fingers loose, he decided to give up the gentle approach. He threw her over his shoulder in a fireman's hold and tried to pass through the narrow doorway.

Once again, Tamara clung to the framework with hands and feet, preventing him from entering the cabin. He used his considerable strength to overpower her efforts and nearly had her past the threshold when she began to fight him with all her might. She kicked and screamed, pummeling his back and thrusting the entire weight of her body against his.

Struggling against the fierceness of her attack, he stumbled backward and lost his balance, causing them both to fall to the ground. Flat on his back, he bore the brunt of the fall, but it took all his strength and coordination to ward off the blows Tamara was aiming at his face and chest.

She fought like a wildcat, kicking and clawing at him with ferocity that was tough to handle, especially since he was determined to keep her from hurting him or herself. There was no opportunity to try calming her with words. She was beyond being consoled by anything he might say, so Rane just let her wear herself out trying to overpower him.

Tamara landed a thudding blow to the side of his face and he grunted in pain, twisting sideways to pin her beneath him and get a firm hold on her flaying fists. He'd almost accomplished his objective when she brought her knee dangerously close to his groin. He automatically shifted from her, allowing her to escape his hold completely. Once free of his confining strength, she scrambled along the ground and tried to put as much distance as possible between them.

Rane quickly recaptured her and halted her flight, but

the fight in her seemed to intensify, not weaken. It was a long, exhausting time later before he had her firmly wedged beneath his massive body. He held her arms tightly and trapped her legs under the muscled weight of his thighs. They were breathing raggedly and they glared at each other with a grimness that declared the battle far from finished.

Rane knew she would renew her attack as soon as he lessened his hold. He'd never fought a woman before and he'd never encountered a man with such obstinacy. His initial assessment of her character was shot to hell. He'd always found Tamara attractive, but he'd thought her somewhat lacking in emotional depth. Instead, she possessed an abundance of fiery passion and gutsy fortitude.

Shallow, emotionless people didn't have the capacity or desire to launch such a bold attack on someone nearly twice their size. Tamara Bennington was no superficial socialite or yuppy executive. This beautiful woman had the tenacity of a pit bull. He decided to move fast and forcefully while she was still trying to catch her breath.

With an economy of motion, Rane rose from the ground and hoisted Tamara over his shoulder again.

"I'm not going in there!" she rasped in a labored tone while pounding his back with furious fists.

She grabbed the door frame when he tried to carry her through the opening, but she didn't have enough energy left to hold out against his superior strength.

As soon as Rane entered the cabin, he felt Tamara go limp in his arms. He carried her to the bed where he carefully laid her down. It was a shock to realize she'd actually fainted.

He sat beside her and brushed the tangle of hair from

her face, studying her closely. Her skin was damp and flushed from exertion. She would probably be stiff and sore with a multitude of bruises by morning. Why the hell had she fought him so fiercely?

She looked peaceful for the moment, but exhausted. Rane couldn't resist stroking a gentle finger over the creamy complexion of her face. Then he lightly tapped her cheek to wake her. He couldn't believe she was so afraid of him. He was big and ugly, but she hadn't been so adversely affected by his presence earlier in the day. Why the sudden fear of entering his cabin? Did she think he intended to ravage her?

As tempting as the idea was, Rane knew without a doubt that he didn't want anything she wasn't willing to give. She intrigued him as few women ever had done, but he was here to protect her. All his protective instincts were aroused by this woman.

Tamara's lashes fluttered and she stared directly into Rane's watchful eyes. His expression was disturbing and she was instantly aware of her prone position and his close proximity.

"What happened?" she asked, remembering their battle and his cautious handling of her as she'd fought with all her strength.

"You fainted," he told her.

"I've never fainted in my life!" she argued, pulling herself into a sitting position, then moaning softly as she felt the tautness of her muscles. "You probably knocked me out!"

Rane's deep, husky laughter echoed about the room and sent a shiver of awareness throughout her body. She was surprised to find such pleasure in the sound of his laughter. If she wasn't careful, she would find herself liking Rane Masters too much.

She knew instinctively that he wasn't the type of man she could share a platonic relationship with. He was a man of deep desires. A woman would have to love him with genuine intensity and Tamara didn't have that kind of emotional courage. She would have to guard against any outbursts of passion.

"No, I didn't hit you, but I was sorely tempted," Rane confessed, feeling a wealth of relief at her spirited accusation. "I think your brain was just trying to give you a break from tension."

"Tension," Tamara repeated, suddenly remembering why she'd panicked. He'd tried to drag her into a dark cabin. *This cabin*, she thought with distress, looking around her with renewed claustrophobia.

"It's so dark and stuffy in here," she managed to whisper, trying to control her fear.

Rane was confused by the abrupt change in her mood, but he reached behind her and touched a button that operated an overhead panel. The massive oak inset slowly slid open to reveal a huge skylight. Gradually, the room was illuminated with the rose-gold glow of late afternoon sunshine.

Tamara gazed at the skylight and slowly relaxed. She told herself that her fears were totally irrational, but she still felt immense relief when the sunlight poured over her.

"Not your average rustic cabin," she declared roughly, fighting off memories of another small, dark mountain home.

Then she noticed how closely Rane was watching her and she automatically lifted her hands to straighten her tousled hair. She knew she must look a mess. She began to smooth her sweatshirt over her torso, then berated herself for her stupidity.

Why should she care what she looked like in the eyes of this man? She was being held against her will and Rane was guilty of kidnapping. She didn't even like the man.

"What now?" she asked irritably, glancing about her to survey the huge, long room that served as both the bedroom and living area. The improved lighting defined the rustic decor with its rather luxurious furnishings. Hardwood floors gleamed beneath brightly-colored throw rugs and a massive fireplace covered the entire end of the building.

She didn't see a television or radio, but there was an elaborate stereo system that confirmed the presence of electricity. The sofa, loveseat, and easy chair were covered with sturdy fabric in hues of brown, orange, and gold. Everything, including an over-large leather recliner, suited the big man beside her.

"I have to check out the electric generator and make sure the water pump is primed," Rane supplied, moving off the bed and putting a safe distance between himself and his enticingly lovely captive. "After I've checked everything, we can eat some dinner."

"And what am I supposed to do?" Tamara snapped. "I have no training in the behavior of a kidnap victim."

Rane suppressed a grin. "You're welcome to look around." He wanted her to be comfortable here. "Just don't stray out of the house. It's not safe to wander about this area alone." He didn't want a resurgence of panic, yet he didn't want her doing anything foolish.

If Rane hadn't turned away, he'd have seen the sparkle of challenge in her eyes. She knew the mountains, they were an integral part of her upbringing and she didn't fear anything she might encounter in the wild. She only feared the isolation.

Nine years ago she'd fought her way off a mountain carrying a four-year-old child. She'd never imagined she might have to make that sort of traumatic trek again, but she knew she didn't lack the ability or determination. She didn't know their exact location, but the only sure way off a mountain was down it.

When Tamara heard the closing of the back door, she eased herself off the bed and followed Rane. Her eyes lit with surprise and delight as she entered the rear portion of the cabin. There was another long room that had been divided into kitchen and bathroom.

The kitchen glistened with shiny surfaces and modern appliances. This was hardly a meager mountain shack. The kitchen was furnished with a sturdy, handcrafted dinette set, and the whole room was bright with color. The white tile floors gleamed. The canary-yellow walls were cheerful, as were the ruffled curtains made from a gaily patterned print.

The bathroom was equipped with equally bright, traditional fixtures. There was a mirrored vanity, a large tub, a shower, and a toilet that flushed. Tamara was amazed to find such features in an isolated cabin. Her memories of mountain existence didn't allow for basic conveniences. Perhaps they weren't too far from civilization.

She wandered around the kitchen and lightly touched each appliance. There was a modern conversion oven with a microwave, a refrigerator, a dishwasher, and a freezer. A glance inside the refrigerator and freezer revealed a stockpile of supplies.

Even the cupboards were crammed with canned goods, spices, and baking supplies. Tamara wondered how long she'd be expected to appreciate the collection of provisions. Not long, she decided confidently, but she would enjoy her brief stay.

She heard noises outside and stepped through the kitchen door to see where Rane had gone. The screened porch that ran the length of the cabin was another pleasant surprise. Late afternoon sun filtered through nearby trees and bathed the room with the warm glow of hominess. The porch furniture was heavy oak, padded with plush, overstuffed cushions, which looked extremely comfortable.

The whole place was lovely and inviting. Tamara tried not to be impressed. She'd be wiser to spend time planning her escape. She had no desire to spend weeks in captivity with Rane Masters.

She could see him moving about in a small building, which adjoined the cabin. It appeared to be a storage shed for the generator and probably the water pump. Her abductor seemed very familiar with this place and she wondered if he'd done any of the designing or decorating. He seemed a man of many talents.

Was he equally adept at kidnapping? So far, he'd been successful, but he didn't seem worried about turning his back on her. She hoped his trusting attitude continued until she'd escaped.

As soon as Rane gave her some leeway, she'd head in the opposite direction. There was a ridge of trees just beyond the back door. It offered a vantage point that topped the cabin's roof and rose above the towering pines for an overall view of the surrounding area. From there she could decide which direction to go. Maybe she'd even spot a highway or nearby town. The angle of the sun promised an hour or so of remaining daylight to accomplish her objective.

Rane left the shed and returned to the house. When

he entered the porch, he saw Tamara standing in the kitchen doorway. She was still dirty and disheveled from their wrestling match, but now her eyes were bright and alert. He seemed to find her more appealing each time he laid eyes on her.

"Are you hungry?" he asked, studying her. She returned his steady gaze and studied him just as intently, although she no longer seemed frightened of him.

"Yes," Tamara said. It had been a long time since her snack on the plane and she would need all the strength she could muster for her escape.

"Did you check the contents of the refrigerator?" he queried, moving past her to the bathroom, acting as though they were casual friends.

"I saw ham and cheese," she replied, deciding to play along with him. If he wanted to pretend there was nothing amiss in this bizarre situation, then she could play the conquered heroine for a little while.

"There's bread in the freezer, if you want to thaw it in the microwave," Rane told her while washing the dust and grime from his hands.

"I'm dirty," Tamara declared, looking at the filth she'd accumulated while rolling on the ground like a Sumo wrestler.

Rane came out of the bathroom and graciously held the door while Tamara moved past him. He found he liked watching her move.

Tamara took advantage of the facilities, using soap, a spare hairbrush, and a soft, absorbent towel that seconded as a cloth to wipe excess dirt from her clothing. She heard Rane moving about the kitchen with easy, economical movements, and she wondered if he did everything with ease and efficiency.

"Beer, cola, or mountain stream water?" he asked her as she reentered the kitchen. He had the table set with several platters of food and was filling one glass with foaming beer.

She found his efforts annoying. She'd pegged him as a chauvinist who'd expect to be catered to. "Just water, thanks," she said, moving past him and seating herself at the table.

Rane sat down opposite her. Their eyes immediately clashed and sexual tension sizzled between them. Tamara felt a jolt of awareness at his nearness. Swallowing hard, she fought her reaction. She couldn't afford an attraction to this man.

She decided to ignore him, and he seemed of the same mind. They ate in silence, then cleared the table. Rane started to load their dirty dishes in the dishwasher, but Tamara stopped him.

"I'll wash the dishes. There's hardly enough to justify wasting electricity," she said, running water in the sink and hoping he'd wander off and leave her unattended. There was barely an hour of daylight left.

Rane studied her suspiciously as she busied herself at the sink. He wanted to believe that she'd resigned herself to the situation, but he didn't trust her. He knew instinctively that she was going to keep fighting him.

He didn't relish another physical confrontation tonight. His curiosity about her had increased, as had his fantasies of making love to her. If she threw herself at him again, he might not be able to handle her with as much care and caution.

"I think I'll go back to the helicopter and get our suitcases," he told her. "I won't be gone long, and I'll be back before it's completely dark. You'd better stay inside. You never know what wild creatures might be stirring outside at this time of night.''

Rane hoped that little warning would give her something to think about while he was gone. Maybe she'd even be glad to see him return. *When pigs fly*, the more practical side of his brain declared, making him grin.

Tamara's lips curved in a wry grin, too. The only wild creature likely to be lurking was her captor. She wasn't fool enough to think the mountains free of wildlife, but she had no intention of encountering or antagonizing any mountain animals.

As soon as the door closed behind him, she moved to the front window and watched until Rane was completely out of sight. Then she hurriedly exited through the back porch door. It was growing dark, but she could still see well enough to climb the ridge opposite the cabin and locate a tall tree that offered several footholds.

It had been years since she'd shinnied up a tree and it was no easy task, but once she reached sturdy limbs, she climbed to a clear vantage point. From there she could see for miles, even in the dusky light.

Rane's cabin set atop a mountain peak. The surrounding mountainside was heavily wooded and the foliage was dense. She could see distant valleys that might be populated. She judged the nearest one to be within five or six miles, but that meant ten or fifteen miles on foot.

It wasn't going to be easy, yet she had no real choice. She had to brave the darkness and the forest. She was determined to go home and she'd use whatever means available to her. There was no telephone at the cabin to reach Harold, so she was left to her own devices. She might not be able to overpower Masters, but she could try to outsmart him.

Getting back down the tree was more difficult than climbing and it took longer than she'd anticipated. Tamara swore softly as she continually lost her footing on the rough bark. She gasped as her descent accelerated and then stifled a scream as she felt herself being grasped by hard, muscled arms. She didn't need a crystal ball to tell her whose big, solid body had cushioned her fall. She didn't even fight her captor as he slowly turned her to face him—and the consequences of her actions.

FOUR

"So," drawled Rane in a gravely tone, his eyes piercing. "All that civility was just camouflage."

Tamara's eyes flashed and her head tilted at a rebellious angle. She refused to respond. Let him guess what he would.

"You're just full of surprises, aren't you?" he continued softly. "Who'd have thought that such a beautiful, petite lady could have nerves of steel and the determination of ten men?"

"I'm not petite," she denied, while trying to worm out of his arms without rubbing any closer to him. The hard, solid warmth of him made her nervous. "You're just overgrown," she argued, hoping the peevish response would conceal her acute awareness of his disturbing masculinity.

Rane's hold on her tightened as he easily lifted her upward and more fully against his body. "I am big," he murmured in a low growl near her ear. "And you'd be wise to remember how strong I am before you pull another stunt like this."

60

Tamara was having a hard time catching her breath, but she blamed it on the tree climbing and the scare she'd had when Rane grabbed her. His mouth whispered across her face from ear to cheek and her breathing became more erratic. She didn't try to analyze the wild excitement building within her.

"I'm going to kiss you," he told her as one big hand slid down her spine to support her hips.

His own pulse thudded heavily in his ears as he absorbed the feel of her. Lowering his mouth to hers, he softly teased the fullness of her lower lip. The first instant of contact was shockingly sweet, and he savored it. He kept a tight rein on the desire to ravage her soft mouth, but allowed himself the pleasure of investigating every tantalizing centimeter of her lips.

Tamara forgot how to breathe. Her body refused all mental commands to withdraw from Rane's sweet seduction.

He wasn't doing anything invasive, but his touch inflamed her. If she enjoyed his slow, tender caresses, he might rapidly become a threat. She forced herself to withdraw from his hold and his marauding lips.

"You made an awfully quick trip to the helicopter," she declared in an annoyingly husky tone.

"I got lonesome," Rane taunted, trying to cool the heat that engulfed his body. He'd never been so quickly and thoroughly aroused by just holding a woman. "I thought I'd better take you with me to help carry some luggage."

Tamara didn't bother to respond, but fell into step beside him. As they skirted the cabin and headed for the helicopter, she decided that silence was her safest recourse.

Rane sensed her resentment, but couldn't tell if she

resented his kisses or if she was just annoyed at being caught up a tree. The embrace he'd enjoyed might not have had any effect on her. He supposed it was stupid to try to coax a reaction from Tamara right now, but her apparent indifference to him was more frustrating than outright hostility. Something about her calm, distant attitude made him want to destroy the barriers she'd always erected between them.

He noticed that Tamara moved over the rough ground with graceful agility. She wasn't totally out of her element here. He'd been wrong to imagine she'd be fearful of stepping outside the protective shelter of the cabin.

Where had she learned to shinny up a tree? How had she known to use the tree as a lookout? And what had she been looking for? Roads? Houses? A means of escape?

She was one clever lady. Still, she couldn't have seen much from her perch. The nearest road was seven miles away and the path to it was long and winding. The nearest town was another ten miles down the road.

When Tamara reached the helicopter, she waited without a word for Masters to give orders. Instead, he handed her one small case and picked up two large ones to carry himself.

"This will be enough for tonight," Rane told her, keeping his tone neutral and trying not to let her aggravating silence get to him. "We can collect the rest tomorrow."

Rane let Tamara lead the way back to the cabin. He noted her increased tension as they plunged through the thick foliage, yet she didn't seem quite as tense as she'd been the first time through. He hoped she wouldn't try anything stupid. She could easily get lost or hurt in this heavy terrain.

As soon as they entered the cabin and put down the suitcases, Rane turned to Tamara and issued a gruff command. "Give me your shoes."

Tamara's eyes widened and she looked at him with an expression of haughty disdain. She understood his reasoning, but resented his clever forethought. By taking away her shoes, he hoped to ensure that she didn't venture too far.

Sitting on the edge of the bed, she tugged off her shoes while Rane switched on several lights to dispel the increasing darkness.

"Why don't I think that will stop you?" Rane asked aloud as he tossed her shoes in an old-fashioned cedar chest that he locked. He gave her another searching glance and grew increasingly annoyed by her attitude. She might not like the situation, but he was trying to save her stubborn hide.

"You might as well relax," he growled. "We're here for an extended vacation whether you like it or not. Maybe we'll both rest easier after we've bathed and gotten out of these filthy clothes. You can have first turn at the bathroom."

Tamara knew this was another method of disarming her. He would probably lock up her dirty clothing and leave her with only her nightwear. She accepted the smallest suitcase from Rane and headed to the bathroom where she confirmed her belief that she had nothing suitable to wear.

When Uncle Harold had packed for her, he'd chosen lingerie from her trousseau. Everything was flimsy and sheer. She growled in irritation, but gladly shed her dirty jeans and sweatshirt.

Taking advantage of the big bathtub, she enjoyed a hot, soothing bath, yet she was ever-conscious of

Rane's proximity. She knew he wasn't going to take advantage of her while she bathed, but even that knowledge annoyed her.

She didn't want to consider any redeeming qualities the man might have. She didn't care if he was polite, well-mannered, and capable of gentleness. She didn't even care if his intentions were somewhat altruistic. She just wanted to put some distance between them. She had to keep her defenses alert.

If she wasn't careful, she'd find herself becoming enthralled by the man who'd literally turned her world upside down and then expected her to behave like a grateful, obedient little lady. She wasn't going to cooperate. She wanted to go home. Once there, she could rationally discuss the situation with Harold and the authorities.

Half an hour later she climbed from the tub, dried herself, and braided her damp hair in a tight French plait. She pulled on the least revealing set of underwear she could find and then topped the beige bra and panties with an apricot negligee that was far too transparent for her peace of mind.

She felt incredibly vulnerable and she fought back the memory of Rane's seductive kiss. This was not a honeymoon, and she had no reason to feel so nervous.

Rane was stretched out in his recliner when Tamara reentered the living room. His imagination had been running rampant and he fought to control the emotions aroused by her flushed, natural beauty. Every muscle in his body constricted and his pulse pounded heavily through his veins. She was gorgeous.

"I'm finished," Tamara forced herself to speak. She'd seen the flash of hot desire in his eyes before he'd managed to control his expression.

Head Hunter

The brief flare of undisguised hunger sent a quiver of distress over her body. Stretched out in the chair, his long, lean frame should have looked relaxed, but he looked dangerous. He was so boldly masculine; and his dark eyes made her whole body tingle with sexual awareness.

She stiffened as he rose from the chair and carefully rid her of the bundle of dirty clothing she was using as a protective shield. He locked her clothes in the chest with her shoes, then grabbed his own suitcase.

"I won't be long," he told her in a tone that was half warning.

Tamara didn't realize that she'd been holding her breath until the bathroom door closed behind him. She tried not to wonder what kind of night-time apparel Rane wore. When an image of his naked, muscled body appeared in her mind, she severely berated herself. Despite his tempting masculinity, she was getting out of this cabin tonight. She had to act fast.

As soon as she heard the shower running, Tamara hurried to a bureau she'd noticed earlier. She jerked open the first drawer and found men's underwear. In a matter of seconds, she'd shed her negligee and pulled on a T-shirt that was long enough to be a dress. She also pulled on a pair of heavy wool socks, then opened the front door and quietly let herself out.

She wished she had some money, but she'd worry about explanations when she reached one of the neighboring properties. There had to be houses within walking distance. She'd seen telephone and electric lines.

Her feet were swift and sure as she recovered the ground she'd taken earlier. Plunging herself into the forest took all her courage. She didn't really fear the elements, but the total darkness and isolation brought on an icy fear she'd never been able to conquer. The only way to survive was to force all the fearful thoughts from her mind and concentrate on escape.

Tamara didn't know what lay ahead of her. She headed in the direction of the power lines, knowing she had to go down the mountain toward a valley if she wanted to find other cabins. She moved over the rough terrain and through dense foliage guided by instinct alone. When all else failed, she depended on her instincts because she had the instincts of a survivor.

The night was dark. Threads of moonlight barely flickered through a thick canopy of tree leaves. But for the first time in her life, Tamara felt protected by the dark. She wished she could believe that Rane wouldn't follow her, but she knew he was as crazy and determined as her.

She grudgingly admired the guy. If what he'd told her about his past was true, then he'd pulled through some rough times and managed to come out on top. She felt a certain empathy with him. He was a survivor, too. He was the type who would willingly take risks and fight for what he wanted. She respected him, although she wasn't too pleased to be engaged in private warfare with such a worthy opponent.

Climbing over a fallen tree trunk, she alarmed a flock of birds that had already roosted for the night. Tamara wished she could hush them, but she dared not slow her movements. She had to keep moving, pressing forward.

Although she had been born and raised in rougher terrain than this, it had been many years since she'd pushed her body to maximum endurance. Weaving around tree trunks and dodging low-hanging branches was demanding exercise, more exhausting than aerobics. Once she was certain she couldn't be trailed, she could set a more reasonable pace, but for now she had to push herself. That man wouldn't be easy to shake.

About a mile into the thickly-wooded forest Tamara stopped to catch her breath and listen. Her own breathing sounded loud in her ears and her lungs burned from exertion. Her body was covered with a fine sheen of perspiration and the night air felt blessedly cool against her flesh.

When her breathing quieted a little, she heard another disquieting chorus of sounds. Someone was close behind her, alarming all the birds she'd just upset. That someone wasn't even trying to be quiet. He was coming after her at a rapid pace. She had to keep moving. Rane's long legs could quickly narrow the gap between them.

Tamara decided to change course. She began to run in a ninety-degree angle from her original downhill plunge. With the added panic of Rane at her heels, she began losing control. Brush and twigs snapped noisily under her feet. She groaned when sharp branches clawed at her bare flesh.

She wasn't really surprised when she heard Rane a few steps behind her, yet she was startled enough to stumble when his huge, hot hands grasped her waist. Rane kept her from falling to the ground, but his grip was scorching. His body, when he pulled her tightly against him, seared her even more.

He was an inferno of heat to her overexposed flesh. His breathing was as ragged as hers and for a few minutes all they could do was cling to one another while battling for air.

When Rane had regained enough breath to speak, he singed the air with oaths that should have shocked her, yet didn't. His hands left her waist and his arms engulfed her quivering body while he continued to berate her for being so foolish. After telling her, repeatedly, how dangerous the forest was and how dumb it was to race down a mountain at night, he finally shook her gently and forced her to look him in the eyes.

"Don't you have any common sense at all?" he rasped. "Why the hell did you try such an idiotic stunt in nothing except underwear? Your skin will be ripped to shreds!"

Tamara didn't utter a word. She still couldn't breathe too well, and she knew nothing she could say would soothe this angry giant. A stream of moonlight allowed her to see the fiery brilliance of his eyes and she returned his gaze with unblinking steadiness, but her lips stayed sealed.

"Damned hardheaded woman," grated Rane irritably. "How the hell could you see where you were going? Most people would have been lost within minutes of entering the forest. And that's in the daytime. You were navigating like a highly-sensitized electronic device."

"Was I headed toward the nearest town?" Tamara finally asked, her eyes alight with satisfaction.

"Are you totally fearless or just insane?" he snapped without answering her question. She didn't need her directions confirmed. "Do you have cat's eyes and animal instincts?"

The thought of animals made Rane tighten his arms about her. He'd imagined all sorts of horrible fates befalling her. He found he couldn't bear the thought of her beautiful skin being flayed or her features contorted in pain. And he was furious with her for scaring him so badly.

"You're crazy, woman!" he accused as he pulled

her even tighter against his chest and enveloped her in a hug that made the air whoosh from her lungs again. It was the only form of punishment he could bring himself to administer.

Tamara's body was damp from exertion and rapidly cooling in the night air. His body was cooling, too, but the feel of her ignited smoldering fires within him. He could feel the tightness of her nipples through the thin fabric of her bra and he struggled with the raw emotions she kindled in him.

He knew he had to get her back to the cabin before she caught pneumonia, but he wanted to drag her to the ground and make hard, feverish love to her. His desire was so fierce that it shocked him and he knew Tamara had to be shocked by the surging evidence of his arousal. Perhaps that's why she was standing so perfectly still, he thought derisively. She was wise enough to remain motionless until he regained control.

"We'd better get back to the cabin before you get too cold." His tone was harsh, but his touch was gentle as he propelled her from him. "It can't be more than fifty degrees out here and you're accustomed to the heat of south Texas."

Tamara retraced her steps with little trouble, amazing Rane with her uncanny sense of direction. He was familiar with the area surrounding his property and had no trouble finding his way, but she didn't even know what state they were in. How was she managing? His curiosity was aroused, yet he knew he didn't have a hope of getting her to supply answers to his innumerable questions.

For Tamara, the trek back to the cabin seemed three times farther and ten times more exhausting than her escape. She'd demanded more of her body today than she had in years, and her strength was diminishing. Sheer willpower kept her moving, but the last few yards were difficult to maneuver and she stumbled several times. She didn't object when strong arms lifted her off the ground and Rane once again carried her over the threshold of the cabin.

He was so big and solid and dependable. She rested her head on his shoulder and forced her mind to go blank while she tried to regain some of her physical stamina.

Rane headed straight for the bathroom and stood Tamara on her feet while he filled the tub with warm water. When he finally let his eyes meet hers, he noted a dawning wariness due to the close confines of the small room. Good. She was wise to be wary of provoking him.

"You've got five minutes to take a bath, get dry, and wrap yourself in a towel. I'll find you something suitable to wear," he said with one last glance at her flushed, enticing loveliness.

The instant the door closed behind him, Tamara felt a resurgence of strength and swiftly stripped off the soggy underwear before stepping into the tub. She gasped as the water stung her cold, battered flesh. The scratches she'd suffered were stinging like crazy, mocking her for attempting to thwart Rane. He was not going to let her run from him.

She was barely warmed when she stepped from the tub and carefully patted herself dry. She'd just hitched the towel around her breasts when Rane returned, looking disturbingly male in nothing except low-slung jeans and the dark, curling hair that clothed his broad chest. He had a magnificent physique and she couldn't help but remember the feel of his hard body crushed intimately close to her own.

Tamara couldn't control the blush that stole over her cheeks. There was something so suggestive about sharing a steamy bathroom with a virile male. She'd never known such intimacy before, and her wanton thoughts intensified the heavy atmosphere.

"You should get warm, too," she muttered to cover her confusion.

Rane would have liked to believe she was genuinely concerned, but he didn't plan to be made a fool again. Twice she'd slipped away and he couldn't be positive she wouldn't keep trying; even dressed in a bath towel. She didn't know the meaning of the word quit. They were going to have to come to some sort of agreement or compromise.

"I'm getting in the shower," he told her, easing her backward until she was seated on the toilet lid. "You're going to stay right where I can see you. Close your eyes if you want, but don't even think of leaving."

Tamara's brows rose in haughty displeasure and she would have argued, but he immediately unsnapped his jeans and she knew he wasn't bluffing. She closed her eyes and felt her blush deepen. Then she clenched her teeth in self-disgust. If she were a little bolder or more worldly, she'd watch him with practiced indifference. She wasn't that experienced.

Rane was glad she kept her eyes closed as he stepped into the shower and quickly ran some tepid water over his body. A smile curved his lips when he turned off the taps, reached for a towel, and noticed that Tamara's eyes were still tightly closed.

He found her fascinating. Some of her hair had escaped the braid and curled in tiny tendrils about her heart-shaped face. Long, lush lashes laid against her flushed cheeks. Her skin was satin smooth and made his fingers itch to touch. Her skin was also marred by several reddening welts and ugly-looking scratches that upset him more than he cared to admit. His movements grew jerky as he hitched the towel around his waist.

"You can open your eyes now," he told her as he stepped from the tub. He watched as her lashes cautiously rose and was amazed at her shyness. Could she be as innocent as she seemed? She'd been engaged, so surely she had some intimate experience with the opposite sex.

"What now?" Tamara managed to ask, trying desperately to ignore his big, virile body. She'd intended her question to be tart, but having him so close made her throat tighten annoyingly.

Her eyes were wary and that annoyed Rane. "Now, we get ready for bed," he clipped, collecting a pile of clean clothes and handing her fresh underwear along with one of his shirts.

"You'll have to settle for this flannel shirt. There doesn't seem to be any practical nightwear packed for you."

Tamara knew that. She cursed her own romantic purchases, feeling exposed by his increasing knowledge of her most intimate belongings. She wanted some privacy, and the pointed glance she gave him said as much.

"I'll dress in the living room." He abruptly left.

Tamara closed her eyes and dragged in a long, calming breath. The man unnerved her more than anyone she'd ever known. Something about him inflamed her sense on a primitive level that she didn't know how to cope with. His presence unarmed her in an elemental fashion that she wasn't prepared to analyze.

His flannel shirt felt good against her skin. It was worn, soft, and very big, but comfortably so. She rolled back the cuffs to fit her arms and fastened the buttons to her neck. Finally, she felt decent enough to exit the bathroom.

Rane was dressed in a pair of worn, faded jeans that hugged his lean hips and accentuated the muscles of his thighs. He was making her hot chocolate, but he was drinking amber liquid from a highball glass.

Rane felt his body tighten at the sight of her in one of his favorite shirts. "I thought you might like something hot to drink," he said.

Tamara sat down at the table and accepted a cup of hot chocolate. It was delicious and the gesture was thoughtful. She thanked him politely.

"You're welcome," he countered with equally guarded politeness. He didn't want to do or say anything that might further heighten the tension between them. His patience was wearing thin.

"Are you done trying to run away tonight?" he asked in a quiet tone.

Tamara was aware that the rein on his control was near the snapping point. She didn't push her luck. "I'm very tired."

Rane's eyes hadn't left her since she entered the kitchen. "You should be totally exhausted," he said. "I am."

Tamara finished her cocoa and carried the cup to the sink. She didn't like his intense scrutiny, but she didn't want to provoke him further, so she kept quiet. She washed the dishes she'd left earlier and cleaned Rane's glass. Neither of them seemed capable of casual conversation.

"It's bedtime," Rane announced, noting the weary droop of her shoulders. "I'll lock up. You can go to bed."

Tamara wished she had the energy to argue, but bed sounded awfully appealing. At least it did until she remembered that there was only one.

Rane anticipated her disapproval. "The sofa opens up into a bed. I had planned to use it, but I don't think it's wise to put that much distance between us tonight."

Tamara really didn't have the energy to argue, but she planted her hands on her hips and prepared to debate the issue.

"We're going to *sleep*," he told her in a no-nonsense tone. "That doesn't mean I don't want you and that I wouldn't like to go to bed with you for purely carnal reasons," he tacked on in a low, husky tone, "but it's not going to happen tonight."

Tamara quivered in response to his blatant honesty and the naked hunger in his eyes. He didn't say it wouldn't happen, only that it wouldn't be tonight. She felt strangely lost, unable to muster an objection.

It was shocking to realize she didn't find the idea of making love with him the least bit repulsive. She wasn't the experienced woman he thought her to be, and she imagined that he would find her inexperience disappointing.

She didn't want him to know how insecure she was when it came to sexual intimacy. He already knew too much about her. If she wasn't very careful, he would breech all her defenses.

Relaxing her belligerent stance, she turned without a word and headed for the other room. Rane wasn't far behind as she approached the bed and leaned over to pull back the covers.

A glance at her long, bare legs and softly rounded hips created even more havoc with his libido. A savage hunger gnawed at his guts.

To combat the feverish desire, he busied himself by making sure Tamara's clothing was locked in the cedar chest. The only thing he didn't lock up was a pair of silk stockings. He didn't know why Harold had packed them, but they would be useful.

Tamara sleepily watched Rane's movements as her body gratefully welcomed the comfort of a firm mattress and fresh, smooth sheets. She frowned when he came towards the bed with a pair of stockings in his hand. She was too tired to think of a logical reason for him to be holding her hosiery.

When he sat on the edge of the bed and reached for one of her legs, she grew more alert. She tried to scramble out of his reach, but she wasn't fast enough.

"What are you doing?" she gasped as he deftly knotted one stocking about her left ankle.

"I'm going to tie you to the bed."

"The hell you are!" she spouted, ineffectively tugging against his hold on her. "That's insane. I thought you were supposed to be protecting me!"

"I can't protect you if you take stupid risks, and I'm too tired to chase you down the mountain again tonight."

Tamara snarled at him as he tugged her closer to the brass rungs of the bed frame. She had no strength left to fight him. Still, she was alarmed at the idea of being completely helpless and incapacitated.

"I can't sleep this way!" Tamara argued in renewed agitation.

FIVE

"You *think* you can't sleep this way. I *know* I can't sleep any other way," Rane countered lightly. "I know you're as tired as I am, yet you've proven that you have to be watched every minute. The only way either of us will get any sleep is if we're tied down."

"We're tied down?" she retorted sharply. He was moving about and she had a leg bound to the bed. Still, if he only tied one leg, it wouldn't be hard to slip away once he was asleep.

Rane knew the wheels of her brain were already spinning thoughts of escape. He'd soon put a stop to those errant schemes. First, he had to administer some first aid to his reluctant captive. He went to the bathroom and returned with some antiseptic cream.

"Slip your arms out of the shirt and lie flat," he told her as he eased himself beside her on the bed.

"Why can't you just leave me alone?" Tamara asked. She knew he'd already seen her in underwear, but she also knew he was fighting to control his physi-

76

cal desire. If sparks between them were re-ignited, she was likely to get burned.

"You have some nasty scratches and I'm not going to let you get a serious infection," he explained.

He leaned closer and she shifted out of his reach. His teeth clenched in irritation. He didn't want to touch her any more than necessary, but she was covered with scrapes she couldn't tend herself. His self-control was already stretched to the limits and her refusal to cooperate made him more testy.

"Take off the shirt, or I'll do it for you."

When she saw the flare of anger in his eyes, Tamara reached for the buttons of the shirt. The process was slow and nerve-racking for both of them. She knew he wasn't going to attack her, but the act of undressing before his watchful eyes made her uncomfortable.

Her modesty and fumbling actions nearly drove Rane to the brink of sanity. He ground his teeth and tried to ignore the unintentional provocation. He just wanted to take care of her and then block the sight and smell of her from his mind.

After slipping the sleeves of the shirt from her arms, Tamara tentatively reached for the ointment, but Rane brushed her hand aside and gently shoved her flat on her back.

Mesmerized by the taut control of his features and the churning emotion in his eyes, Tamara lay as still as possible. His big body communicated a warning that she was careful to heed. Strangely enough, she trusted him, yet she didn't push her luck.

Rane kept his touch light and impersonal as he dabbed cream on her slim arms. She had several marks on her neck and shoulders where he carefully smoothed salve. One nasty-looking scratch made an ugly welt in the rounded firmness of her right breast, just above her bra. He gently touched the tempting softness, then quickly instructed her to turn over.

Tamara obeyed his hoarse command without a whimper of protest. The feel of his slowly stroking fingers was melting every bone in her body. She was holding her breath and noted that Rane's breathing was getting more shallow. When he'd finished her back, she turned over again, her eyes flying to his in wary regard.

There was a nasty scrape on her abdomen, and Rane gave it his attention next. He admired her smooth, flat stomach and her satin softness, but his jaw tightened when she flinched at his touch. He was furious with himself for letting her get hurt.

Such an exquisite body should be pampered, not battered and bruised. He hated the thought of anything hurting her, especially his touch, and he was shocked by the strength of his protective instincts. He'd never met a woman who inspired protective and possessive emotions as turbulent as his feelings for Tamara.

He determinedly ignored the soft mound that was enhanced rather than concealed beneath sheer bikini panties. Tamara turned so that he could take care of the leg that was tied, but he checked it and moved to her right leg. The last area needing attention was her silken thigh.

Rane's fingers grew more tender as he spread soothing ointment over this section of her leg. He wanted to follow the path of his fingers with his mouth and kiss it all better, but he fought the urge. Then he abruptly rose from the bed and took the antiseptic back to the bathroom.

Tamara expelled a heavy sigh when he left the room. She felt as though she'd just tiptoed through a mine field. Her breasts were swollen and her nipples tight with aching. The gentle touch of Rane's calloused fingers had left her body pulsing with a need unlike anything she'd ever experienced. She never would have believed that any man's touch could create such havoc on her body.

She rebuttoned the shirt much faster than she'd undone it. Her fingers trembled, and her relief was enormous. She was growing altogether too fascinated with her captor.

She'd never met a man who made her feel so desirable, yet so wary of that desire. She had a feeling that Rane Masters would be a tender, but demanding and passionate lover. She was afraid that making love with him would threaten her emotional well-being and drastically change her life.

When Rane returned, he switched off the light and tugged off his jeans. He didn't own any pajamas, so Tamara would have to get used to seeing him in his briefs.

Tamara was on the left side of the bed and he climbed in the right side. She tensed when he reached for her and he cursed under his breath. He used the remaining silk stocking to bind her right wrist to his left one, insuring that she wouldn't leave the bed without waking him.

"I can't sleep on my back," she offered one last daring argument against confinement. She ignored the jolt of fiery sensation where their skin touched.

"You'll have to tonight," he told her. They were both so exhausted they could probably sleep upside down. If he could just put the thought of loving his adorable captive out of his mind, then he might be able to get some rest.

"Do you want me to close the skylight?" Rane asked as he pulled a comforter over them.

"No!" Tamara responded. The view of diamond bright stars against a black-velvet sky calmed her. "I like it open."

"I like it open, too," murmured Rane. He had to get some rest and break the spell she'd cast over him. After a good night's sleep, he'd be more in control and better prepared to cope with her enchanting loveliness.

"Good night, Tamara," he couldn't keep the possessive huskiness from his tone.

Tamara responded sleepily. She was very much aware of him, but she was lulled by the comfort of the bed and the star-spangled beauty of the sky. Her lashes fluttered, her eyelids drooped and she relaxed for the first time in hours. Within minutes, she was asleep.

For Rane, sleep was harder to find. But once he'd commanded his body to ignore the temptation of his bedmate, he slept deeply.

Toward morning, when he was fully rested, Rane began to dream vivid dreams of the lady sharing his bed. As he slowly awakened from his fantasies, his mind and body registered the fact that a very warm, very soft woman was pressed close to his side. The heat of her body scorched him from shoulder to thigh. He opened his eyes, squinting slightly as the early morning sun shone through the skylight. Then he turned his eyes to Tamara.

She was still sleeping soundly and in nearly the same position she'd fallen asleep. Rane momentarily regretted having tied her to the bed, yet she didn't appear harmed by his precautionary measure.

He seemed to have done all the restless shifting

throughout the night. The arm that was tied to Tamara's was stretched over her head and the rest of his body had snuggled closer to her womanly warmth. He carefully raised his right hand to untie the knot about their wrists, leaving his hand free to touch the top of her head.

Her hair was still bound in a braid, but a riot of curls resisted the confinement and softly framed her face. She looked so young, innocent, and lovely in slumber. Long, thick lashes rested against her creamy cheeks. Rane's heart rate quickened as he studied her fragile beauty.

One short scratch and a darkening bruise over her left temple were the only imperfections on her ivory-smooth complexion. He was amazed at the distress those marks caused him. This independent lady brought out aspects of his character that he wasn't aware he possessed.

His concern for her kept growing, and he wasn't sure he welcomed those feelings. He was trapped in a situation of his own making, but he didn't want to be free of his responsibility until he'd had plenty of time alone with Tamara.

Brushing his thumb lightly over one of her cheeks, he was awed by the tenderness that welled within him. Compared to his massive size, she was just a little thing; yet so spirited, courageous, and desirable. He wanted to possess her in the most elemental fashion.

He'd fought this strong attraction since the first time he'd laid eyes on her. Yet now that he knew her better, it was more than a physical attraction. The need in him had become emotional, as well, and he wanted her to need him with the same intensity.

He stroked her jaw, and then cupped the side of her

face in his big palm. Without considering his actions, Rane leaned his head down and pressed his mouth gently against her slightly parted lips. He wanted to wake her with kisses. He continued to ply her mouth with soft caresses, using his lips and tongue to tease her.

Tamara's eyes fluttered open to the sight of Rane's face so close to her own. Her lips tingled where his touched them. Her pulse quickly accelerated from slow and slumberous to wild and erratic. Sensual awareness began to wash over her body in steady waves of sensation. Her eyes widened, meeting Rane's in an unblinking stare that assured him she recognized his hunger.

"What do you want from me?" she asked in drowsy demand, hotly aware of the hard length of him pressed against her side.

"I want to make love to you," he answered softly.

Their eyes locked in an intense, soulful stare.

"But you're not going to, are you?" she insisted, knowing he wouldn't take her against her will.

"Not unless you want the same thing," Rane replied huskily as he stole another kiss, trying to make her want him as badly as he wanted her.

Tamara felt the tightly-leashed hunger in him being transmitted to her. His tender assault on her mouth was potent. She grew restless and yearned to touch him, but commonsense warned her not to arouse a passion she couldn't satisfy.

When Rane's mouth left hers, it traveled along her cheek to her ear and then down her neck to the pulse throbbing wildly at her throat. Chills danced over her body. How could this man's touch create such intense longing in her?

She'd never been impressed or aroused by any man's deliberate attempts to seduce her. Yet no man had ever shared the wide range of emotions she'd experienced in the past twenty-four hours. She'd never let any man close enough to really threaten her composure. Something about Rane's tenderness tempted her to abandon herself completely and that was scary.

"Good morning, Ms. Bennington," Rane murmured as he appreciated the way the sunlight shimmered over her sleep-flushed features, making her look sweet and soft and unbelievably desirable.

His possessive tone brought warmth to Tamara's face. The gleam in his eyes was equally unsettling. No amount of smooth-tongued compliments had ever affected her like his huskily spoken greeting.

"You're a dangerous man, Rane Masters," she told him in a tone still groggy from sleep. She'd always known that he was dangerous, a man to be avoided at all costs.

Rane's rugged features softened into a slow, sexy smile. "You needn't be afraid of me. I only want to share my body with you." His hands reached for her. His left hand smoothed the hair from her face while the right hand caressed her shoulder.

Tamara's blush deepened at his bold declaration and heat pulsed throughout her body. He didn't need to tell her what he wanted, she felt it in every nerve ending. His hands were calloused, but gentle and ever so exciting.

"I hardly know you," she felt compelled to remind him. She was annoyed by the continued huskiness of her voice and realized that her declaration wasn't strictly true. She felt she knew more about this giant, provocative man than she'd known about Skip, the man she'd been engaged to marry.

Their bizarre relationship had a great deal to do with

the affinity between them. She'd learned that Rane was strong, determined, and self-confident. She also knew he was considerate and capable of fierce loyalty. Like it or not, he intrigued her.

"I want us to get to know one another better," Rane spoke quietly as he nuzzled the tender skin beneath her chin. "And I promise not to do anything that might hurt you."

Tamara started to argue, but he silenced her with a finger over her lips. Then his hand trailed down her throat to the bare flesh at the vee of her borrowed nightwear. He slowly began to unfasten the buttons. Then he laid the shirt front open and exposed her creamy flesh. Clothed in little more than scraps of silk, she was exquisitely lovely.

Tamara's pulse pounded so loudly in her ears that she was deafened to any mental warnings of caution. Her skin caught fire where his eyes touched her and heat more scorching than she'd ever known coursed throughout her body. She should halt his sensual assault. But curiosity, anticipation, and increasing excitement kept her still while Rane's hands and eyes explored her body.

The increased tempo of her breathing made her chest rise and fall in escalating agitation. With each breath, her breasts tautened against the confinement of her bra. Her nipples tingled with the sweet ache of heightened sensitivity. When Rane's roaming fingers lightly brushed them, they hardened instantly.

He leaned closer so that his tongue could tease one taut peak while his thumb stroked the other, and Tamara gasped in violent reaction. Her hands flew to his head, her fingers locking in his thick, tousled hair.

"Rane!" her cry of outrage sounded more like a

husky endearment. She tugged on his hair, trying to shift him long enough to catch her breath and come to terms with the shocking response he was eliciting from her body.

Rane withdrew his mouth from her rigid nipple, leaving a damp spot that continued to tantalize the sensitive flesh. He gently brushed the other nipple with his lips while she began to pull harder at his hair.

He grasped both of her wrists in one large hand; then pulled her arms above her head and held them out of his way. He didn't want her touching him just now, and he didn't want any interference while he explored the rest of her lovely body.

Tamara gasped as he stretched her arms over her head and left her feeling incredibly exposed and vulnerable. He wasn't holding her tightly, yet for some reason she didn't resist him. She did gasp as his free hand began to caress the smooth expanse of her midriff. His touch was hot, yet gentle and mindful of her scratches. His complete absorption in his adoration of her body boggled her mind. No man had ever been granted unconditional freedom to explore her, and her flesh burned with each new caress.

Rane grew increasingly excited by the feel of Tamara and the way she allowed him to proceed. She could have pulled her hands free, yet she wasn't playing games or pretending she didn't enjoy what he was doing. It was obvious that she liked his tentative attempts at lovemaking, even though she was shocked by his audacity.

His eyes met hers as his fingers grazed the welt on her abdomen. She flinched and his troubled gaze told her he shared the brief pain. Releasing her wrists, he slid lower in the bed and touched his lips to the deep abrasion, attempting to kiss away the pain. Tamara quivered in response to his light caress and his control slipped dangerously.

He hadn't intended to make any physical demands on her, but his body was begging for release. He caught her hips in his hands and buried his face in the warm cradle of her thighs, softly nuzzling her through the silk of her panties.

Tamara struggled to catch her breath as liquid heat coursed through her. She clutched at Rane's hair again and pulled him upward until his face rested near her heaving breasts. She felt as though she'd run a marathon and she fought to regain some control, but Rane's lips began a renewed assault on her highly-sensitized nipples and she cried out in desperation.

"Please, no more, you have to stop!" she rasped, her heart thudding painfully in her chest as she felt every inch of his hard, virile body sliding over her trembling form.

"I don't want to stop." He argued roughly, his own breathing ragged. Her wild response to his touch inflamed him as nothing else could have done. His hands kneaded the velvet-smooth skin of her waist, while his mouth nibbled at the turgid tips of her breasts and he rubbed his throbbing body gently against her thighs.

Tamara was drowning in waves of exquisite, erotic sensation. She wasn't totally inexperienced, but no man had ever aroused her to such a fever pitch of desire. Was she losing her mind as well as her self-control? Did she dare to give this man that kind of hold over her?

"Rane, please!" She couldn't risk such devastating

emotional involvement, so she decided to beg. "Please, stop!"

The infinitesimal note of panic in her tone brought Rane's eyes level with hers. She was flushed with excitement and her eyes were glazed with arousal, yet he also detected a hint of real fear.

Shock rippled over his body. He quickly argued the absurdity of her harboring fears of intimacy. She'd been engaged to be married. His eyes held hers while he slowly slid a hand down her body to cup the soft mound between her legs. When he caressed her, she trembled convulsively, but there was still fear in her eyes. He drew in a deep, tortured breath and asked her why.

"Are you afraid I'll hurt you?" He was a big man.

Tamara lowered her lashes, blocking out the disturbing intensity of his dark eyes. How could she tell him she wasn't afraid of him physically, but that his tenderness seared her very soul and the unselfishness of his loving left her totally defenseless? She couldn't handle that sort of vulnerability.

"I'm not afraid of you," she finally managed, reopening her eyes.

"Are you afraid of men in general? Physical intimacy? Social disease? Pregnancy?" He was grasping at straws and simultaneously trying to control his raging desire.

The mention of pregnancy made Tamara's eyes go wider with fear. She'd always been certain that no man could make her irresponsible enough to risk pregnancy. It was a brutal shock to realize she'd been wrong. Rane Masters was a threat to her in more ways than he'd ever know.

"I'm not protected."

Rane closed his eyes and moaned. "You were going to be married."

Tamara grimaced. "I saw a doctor for birth control, but I stopped worrying about it when I canceled my wedding plans."

Rane's groan was low and pained. He'd never brought a woman to this cabin and he didn't carry that kind of protection with him. He had no way to prevent an unwanted pregnancy.

Rolling to his own side of the bed, he threw an arm over his eyes and willed his body to relax. It wasn't easy. His body didn't want to relax. He couldn't remember ever wanting a woman as desperately as he wanted Tamara, yet he'd committed himself to keeping her safe. Harold trusted him and he had a debt of honor to repay. How the hell was he going to cope?

The more Rane got to know Tamara, the more he understood how a man—any man—could become obsessed with her. She was a rare treasure with the heart, soul, and spirit of a tigress wrapped in sweet modesty and stunning sex appeal.

When Tamara's breathing quieted and her body temperature began to cool, she dared a glance at Rane. His breathing had slowed, but she could still see the tension in his big body. The muscles in the arm thrown over his face were tightly coiled and his chest heaved with the strain of reining his passion.

She didn't know a lot about men, but she knew he was having more difficulty dampening his desire than she was. She hated being the cause of such discomfort, but she hadn't been the one to initiate the seduction.

Still, if Rane had been the sort of egotistical tough guy she'd originally thought him, he wouldn't have hesitated to take advantage of her. Another glance at the width of his chest and size of his powerful arms convinced her that she wouldn't have a hope of stopping him if he decided to ravage her.

Her own body had turned traitor. Never in her life had she been so wildly aroused and deprived of common sense. The blush that was starting to recede made an encore over her face and throat. She'd always prided herself for being levelheaded, yet less than ten minutes of Rane's loving had reduced her to a mass of quivering need.

She'd often imagined she was frigid, but his tender, erotic lovemaking wiped that misconception right out of her mind. She knew the big man beside her would make the experience something devastatingly special. Tamara Jo Bennington didn't want to be devastated. She wanted full control of her life and emotions.

"Are you going to be all right?" she asked as she pulled the sides of her shirt closed and fastened the buttons. She tried to look at his bare torso without reacting, but she wasn't successful.

Rane lowered his arm and turned his head toward her. He was surprised and pleased by her innocent query, but his answer was derisive.

"I'll live," he clipped, "but I won't be all right."

His irritable quip brought a tiny smile to Tamara's lips. "I never promised you a rose garden," she commented, unable to contain the absurd lyric that popped into her mind.

Rane was so amazed by her comic retaliation that he turned fully toward her and studied her expression. Tamara shrugged her shoulders in a gesture that proclaimed her inability to explain the origin of the dry humor.

The dismissive shrug added to his amusement and he

began to laugh as he hadn't laughed in years. The sound was contagious and soon Tamara joined in his celebration of their bizarre situation. The sexual tension between them gradually dissipated.

When Rane's laughter softened to a deep chuckle, Tamara gave him a smile that was genuinely warm. He'd been so tender and yet strong enough to protect her. She could no longer think of him as a stranger or a criminal, even though she knew he was a real threat to her peace of mind.

"Where do we go from here?" she asked in a light, but serious tone.

Rane's eyes narrowed as he trapped her with piercing regard. "That depends on you," he declared in equal seriousness.

"How so?" she asked. "Are you willing to take me home?"

"I made your uncle a promise and I intend to keep it. He doesn't want you home until Tralosa's trial is over."

Tamara gave his words careful consideration. If she stayed here she might be safe, but what would her tormentor do if she just disappeared? If someone really wanted to hurt her, what would they do when they couldn't find her? Would they go after her family? She'd been so caught up in her own problems that she hadn't given enough thought to the possibility.

"What are the options?"

"We stay here."

Tamara grew angry again. She didn't like being told what to do and she didn't like the idea of forced confinement.

"I don't want to stay here. You know as well as I do that staying here together is asking for trouble. We can make other arrangements for my protection in San Antonio. If I'm home by Monday, nobody will question my whereabouts this weekend.''

''Harold intends to explain that you've taken an extended vacation. We're not going back to San Antone.''

He sounded far too arrogant and domineering. Tamara's temper simmered and she had an urge to sock him in the jaw. Her fingers curled into balls and she glared at him while mentally reminding herself that ladies do not fight with their fists.

Rane understood her fury and frustration, but couldn't ignore the opportunity to insure her cooperation. ''I'm a whole lot bigger and stronger than you are,'' he warned in a low drawl, his eyes searing her. ''Don't start anything you can't finish.''

Tamara continued to glare at him until he shifted closer. Suddenly, she was trapped under his big body with only his strong forearms protecting her from his crushing weight.

The heat of his body scalded her and sent her senses into a tailspin. His cotton briefs were the only covering on his body except for masses of dark hair. He was so big and hard and virile that he literally stole her breath.

SIX

"You're deliberately trying to intimidate me," Tamara accused.

"I'm trying to make you understand just how volatile this situation is," he countered gruffly. "I made a promise and I intend to keep it. Now, you can either cooperate or we can continue to play games. But I'm warning you right now that I'm real short on patience and self-control."

"Sexual blackmail?" Tamara dared, knowing it would infuriate him. She felt his whole body tighten in anger.

Rane could hardly believe she was taunting him. Few men in his acquaintance had ever dared to provoke him and no woman had ever taken such a risk. Maybe his gentle handling had made her feel a little too safe.

"I want a compromise," he insisted roughly. "You stop trying foolhardy escape plans and I'll promise not to force my attentions on you."

It was a form of blackmail, yet Tamara knew his

attentions wouldn't be a threat if she didn't find him so damned appealing. She wanted to be angry, but the feel of him was doing crazy things to her senses.

Rane had her arms pinned to the bed on either side of her head and his face was tantalizingly close. The tempo of her breathing grew ragged. She felt his muscled strength and the rock-hard width of his chest. The unmistakable evidence of his desire was pressing against her thighs and their bodies were too hot for comfort. The musky scent and masculine feel of him made her senses reel. How could he swear to leave her alone when his hunger was so evident?

"I didn't say it would be easy," he ground out, reading her thoughts. He wanted her badly, but he wanted to bind her to him in more practical ways. He couldn't take the chance that she might get seriously hurt and tying her to the bed wasn't a viable solution. He wanted her to promise she'd behave.

"I would like to make love to you," he continued, watching her eyes as the impact of his statement registered, "but I don't want to take advantage of the situation. I'm not going to take you home and the desire isn't likely to lessen. The only solution is to avoid physical confrontations and control any flare of passion."

"We can do that?" She meant to sound skeptical, but her voice was soft and breathless.

Rane closed his eyes and rested his forehead against hers. A shudder rippled over his body. The battle for control was foreign and alarming. He couldn't remember ever wanting a woman this much. He'd never been so deeply affected by wide, warm eyes and a husky voice. He was sinking in a quicksand of sensations.

Tamara was a little awed by his battle for control. She'd never been the type of woman who made men lose their heads, nor had she ever felt such conflicting emotions of wanting and yet fearing that need. Rane Masters had her totally confused and bemused. He made her feel incredibly special. He made her feel things she didn't want to feel.

"I want your promise that you won't try to run away again," Rane finally insisted when his eyes reopened and locked with hers.

Tamara knew she should try to pacify him. She could make a promise she didn't intend to keep, but her own sense of honor wouldn't allow the lie. Besides, if she succeeded in escaping, she wouldn't have to worry about any retaliation or physical confrontations.

"What about my family?" she hedged.

Rane's big body grew more tense and his eyes flared. She just didn't know when to quit. "I have men guarding your family around the clock."

Alarm widened Tamara's eyes further. "You think they're in danger? Do you really believe someone might hurt my family to get at me?"

"I told you, they're being protected. They don't make targets of themselves like you did. They're a whole lot safer with you out of the way."

Tamara gave that some thought. It was probably true. If someone kept making attempts on her life, one of her loved ones might get involved in the next accident.

"I never thought of that," she whispered. "Until the last attempt, I really hadn't accepted the fact that someone might want to kill me."

Rane felt her tremble and offered comfort without considering the consequences. He eased his arms beneath her and held her tightly for a few minutes, but the feel of her warm, womanly body soon became a threat to his composure. He rolled to his own side of the bed, breathing deeply. That wasn't far enough, so he rose from the bed and strode to the kitchen.

Tamara felt bereft. Without the heat of Rane's body, she was instantly chilled. Closing her eyes, she forced herself to relax. She wasn't a total innocent. She'd been held and kissed by men, even passionately kissed. But when Skip had come close to losing control, it had only irritated her. She'd never allowed herself to lose control. She'd never met a man capable of making her lose control.

Rane drew a glass of cold water and drank thirstily. He ran his hands through his hair and then paced the kitchen until he'd calmed down and could breathe normally. The fire gradually cooled in his bloodstream and he felt capable of returning to the bedroom.

Tamara untied the silk from her ankle and stretched her stiff muscles. Then she forced herself to do something constructive, making the bed while debating about whether she should enter the kitchen.

Rane came in the room and pulled on a pair of jeans. He unlocked the cedar chest so that Tamara could get to her clothes. Then he noticed that the bed was made and allowed his eyes to meet her's.

"Are you ready for some breakfast?"

His tone was carefully polite and she responded in the same fashion. "Breakfast sounds like a good idea."

"I'll cook some bacon and eggs while you get dressed," Rane said. "How would you like your eggs?"

"Any way."

"I'm better with scrambled," he told her.

"Scrambled is fine."

Rane nodded and left the room. Tamara heaved a sigh. Then she collected a clean pair of jeans and a cotton shirt. She headed for the bathroom where she washed, dressed, and rebraided her hair. The enticing smell of frying bacon finally lured her to join Rane in the kitchen.

"The coffee's ready," he said, looking very capable as he stood at the stove and cooked breakfast.

Tamara poured them both a cup and set the table. She found a loaf of bread he'd taken from the freezer and made some toast. In a matter of minutes, they were sitting down to eat.

Everything tasted delicious and Tamara ate hungrily. Rane ate twice as much, but he was twice as big. Together, they polished off a pound of bacon, half-a-dozen eggs, and several slices of toast.

The coffee even tasted special to Tamara. Perhaps it was the mountain water, she mused as they both sipped their second cup in comfortable silence. Perhaps it was due to her heightened senses. The sun seemed brighter, the air cleaner, the food especially tasty. She heaved a deep, relaxed sigh and managed a warm smile for Rane.

"Breakfast was delicious. I could get spoiled."

Rane's eyes studied his guest. Her hair was pulled tightly back from her face, emphasizing the stark beauty of her features. Despite a small bruise and an absence of makeup, she was still the most beautiful woman he'd ever known. Her eyes were big and bright and alight with intelligence. Her nose was straight, her lips full and perfectly bowed. Her smooth skin glowed with health.

"You look more relaxed than I've ever seen you," he commented, realizing that it was a lack of tension that softened her beauty and made her so appealing.

At first, Tamara was surprised by his observation, then she gave the comment some serious thought. She was relaxed. This was the first time in months that her whole body wasn't tight with tension and her brain plagued with responsibilities. It felt good. Her career, personal problems, and the death threats had taken their toll on her nerves.

"I'll bet you've been suffering all the classic problems of a stressed-out executive," Rane continued. "You've probably had a lot of headaches lately, your stomach has begun to revolt, and you aren't getting much sleep. You need a vacation. Your health is more important than all other aspects of your life."

Tamara lowered her eyes to her coffee cup. He was right. She'd known she was pushing herself too hard, but it seemed easier than coping with private disappointment and frustration.

"What makes you such an authority on the subject?" she asked lightly.

"I've been there," Rane admitted. "When I was running the air-transport business, I worked eighteen-hour days until I nearly collapsed." After being freed from that godforsaken Mexican prison, he had been driven by guilt, rage, and an unrelenting need to make his father's dream a reality.

Her soft brown eyes met his. "What did you do?"

"I retired and delegated control to capable managers. I bought this cabin and lived here until my mind and body healed. I'm still president of the company, but I don't run it."

"And that doesn't bother you? To allow others complete control over your family business?" Tamara couldn't imagine it.

"I love ranching," Rane explained. "It's hard work and the hours are long, but the responsibilities are different. I have loyal, trustworthy people working for me if I want time off.''

Tamara gave his words serious consideration. She had two assistant managers who were intelligent and competent. Each department of her store had supervisors she respected and trusted. The company wouldn't fall to ruin if she didn't go to work. Her staff might even thrive on the opportunity to prove their capabilities.

''Nobody's irreplaceable?'' The thought made her a little sad and vulnerable.

Rane smiled slightly, knowing how she felt. He thought she might well be irreplaceable, but he didn't say so. ''It's time you took care of yourself, first.''

That brought a small frown. Tamara didn't know if she could exist without her work. For most of her life, work and family had been the whole of her existence. The one time she'd dared to explore a private life, with Skip, she'd experienced abysmal failure. She wasn't good at coping with failure.

''I'm not sure I know how to relax,'' she admitted, giving Rane a bold, unflinching stare.

''If you give it a chance, it comes naturally.''

Tamara considered his words. She certainly felt relaxed this morning, but the past twenty-four hours had been anything but relaxing. Still, she'd left her normal environment and that seemed to have drained a lot of tension.

''Maybe I do need a vacation,'' she murmured softly.

Rane felt tension drain from his body. There was just a slight chance that she might decide to cooperate with him.

''You won't find a better place to heal.''

Tamara's eyes narrowed. He was mistaken. She

hated the isolation of the mountains and she suffered from old wounds that could never heal. Still, his cabin was a far cry from the shack of her childhood memories and Rane was definitely an attractive incentive to spend time here. She found him utterly irresistible.

"You don't have a telephone or radio," came her weak argument.

"A telephone is the last thing you need, and there's a radio in the helicopter."

"I need to keep in touch with my family," she insisted. "I can't relax if I have to worry about them continuously."

"An employee of mine, Dave Andrews, can fly in here and bring taped recordings from your family. He's due to drop one tomorrow. Then you can tape a response, let them know you're fine, and still enjoy a vacation."

It sounded feasible. Tamara was alarmed at how badly she wanted to accept the arrangements he'd made. He and Harold seemed determined to secure her peace of mind.

She began to shake her head back and forth. "I just can't do it. I can't stay away from home that long."

"Not even for your Uncle Harold?" Rane was forced to use a little emotional blackmail.

"Uncle Harold will understand when I go home and explain how I feel," Tamara insisted.

"You're wrong," replied Rane, rising from his chair. He left the room and returned shortly carrying a white envelope.

Tamara recognized the stationery as soon as Rane handed it to her. She'd given it to her uncle last year for Christmas. Dreading his message, she read the letter.

Dearest Tamara,

You're the daughter of my heart and I love you more than you will ever know. I couldn't bear to have any harm come to you. It would destroy Lucy, Katie, and me. I must protect my family.

I know by the time you read this that you will be adamant about returning home, but I beg you to reconsider. I've never asked a favor or felt that you owed me in any way, but now I'm going to prey on your love and loyalty by asking you to cooperate with Rane and me. Stay with him. Take a well-earned vacation.

Love,
Harold

Tamara read the letter twice. It sounded just like Harold and his handwriting was as familiar as her own. She had no doubt that he'd written the brief, poignant message.

How could she ignore her uncle's plea? She owed him so much and she loved him dearly, but why did he have to ask for favors now? Why wasn't he allowing her an opportunity to present her arguments?

Did he think she was too selfish to honor his wishes? Had she become too selfish of late? Had she been so wrapped up in her own problems that she'd become inconsiderate of those she loved? What now? As Rane had noted earlier, she really had only one option: to stay here.

"You promise I'll be able to stay in contact with Katie?" She looked him straight in the eye.

Rane hardly dared to breathe. The myriad of expressions that had danced across her face were too conflicting to decipher.

His reply was strong and firm. "You have my word, if you promise not to try to run away again."

"And you'll swear there won't be a repeat of this morning's seduction?" Warmth invaded her face, but she had to ask.

"I'm not a eunuch." Rane's voice was low and his eyes penetrating. He watched Tamara's flush darken. "But I swear I won't pressure you or take any stupid risks."

Intuition told Tamara she could trust him, commonsense said that spending time with him was a risk, yet her heart insisted that she stay and explore the unique feelings she'd developed for her self-professed protector.

"I guess we have a deal as long as you keep your promise and allow me to stay in touch with my family."

Relief washed over Rane. He knew Tamara would be staying against her better judgment, yet her decision proved that she was anxious to explore a personal relationship.

"Tammy, is it true?" Katie's high-pitched squeal came off the recording, loud and clear. "Everyone is saying you eloped with Rane Masters. You're the talk of the town!"

Tamara quickly flipped the switch to cut off the teen-age voice and turned to glare at Rane. Hands on hips, eyes flashing, she was ready to fight, but his shocked expression stole some of the wind from her sails.

"You had nothing to do with it?" she demanded, seeing the truth on his face but needing to hear it from him. "This isn't part of your cute little game plan?"

The surprise in Rane's eyes slowly gave way to a calculating gleam. Tamara didn't like it at all.

"I swear I had nothing to do with any speculation about marriage. I didn't think anyone saw me carry you on the plane."

"Won't your friends, family, and employees all suspect where we are now?"

"Andrews is the only person who knows I own this place. Your uncle doesn't even know the exact location."

"So they won't think of this as a honeymoon hideaway?" she asked in disgust.

"They may know I took you somewhere, but there's no way they can find us. Since I didn't tell anyone I was getting married, they won't pay much attention to the rumors."

She believed him. "But?" She knew that something had clicked in his mind. The gossip about an elopement wasn't causing him any distress.

"But it might work to our advantage," he suggested carefully, crossing his arms over his chest.

"Advantage?" Tamara growled, simmering with frustration. "What kind of an example am I setting for Katie? She either thinks I've gone off for an elicit affair with a man I barely know, or she believes that I've been totally irresponsible by eloping. What about Skip? He'll be humiliated. He'll think I was cheating on him long before I called off the wedding. What about my employees? They'll think I've lost my mind entirely!"

Rane fought the grin that tugged at his lips. She was delightful when she was ranting. Her cheeks were flushed and her eyes sparkled with passionate intensity.

"This is not funny, Masters!" Tamara snapped, stopping her agitated pacing to stand in front of him. He wasn't openly laughing at her, but his eyes were alight with amusement.

"I'm not amused by the situation," he explained, then went out on a limb. "I just find you absolutely adorable." He held his breath while she digested the compliment.

Tamara blinked and stared at him in confusion. Why did his words make her heart flutter and her arguments seem trivial? He had to be insane. Nobody had ever used such a ridiculous adjective to describe her. Adorable? Wasn't that for kittens and puppies and babies?

"Adorable?" she found herself repeating the word inanely.

"Absolutely adorable and incredibly lovable," Rane reiterated softly, wondering at her amazement. She acted as though she'd never gotten a genuine compliment from a man.

Tamara was used to compliments. She'd been told she was beautiful and desirable by lots of men. Skip had told her frequently that he found her sexy and gorgeous, yet she related those compliments to physical attributes. Love and adoration were soft, intimate feelings and leaned dangerously close to emotional entanglement.

"I don't think I want to be adorable," she insisted.

Rane was amazed by her reaction and even more amazed at his own lapse of caution. He knew how to shock her out of her worried dissection of his compliment. "I think a rumor about an elopement could prove invaluable to our situation.

"I know you won't agree," he offered sardonically, "but marriage to me might be the perfect form of protective custody."

Tamara blushed at the idea. Her heart refused to stop

the ridiculous fluttering. She couldn't let her imagination run rampant. Rane was just teasing her and she had no intention of taking him seriously.

"What do you mean?" she demanded.

Rane found himself warming to the idea of making her his wife, if only for protective purposes. "Tralosa knows me well. We've kept close watch over each other over the years. He knows I hate him, but that I operate within the confines of the law. He also knows I would take him down with the slightest provocation."

Tamara was mesmerized by the raw emotion that briefly flickered over Rane's rugged features. For an instant, he looked ruthlessly dangerous. A shudder ran down her spine. She was glad he didn't have any old scores to settle with her. He would be a frightening opponent, even for a man like Tralosa, who thrived on violence.

"And you think Tralosa would forget little old me if I was married to big, strong you?" She flirted with danger and tugged at the tiger's tail.

Rane's eyes narrowed. His insides went wild when she challenged him. Damn, she was bold, but her fearless taunting assured him that she wasn't afraid of him. She captivated him with her courage, not just her feminine wiles. She was ready to do battle at his level. That was rare for women in his acquaintance.

"I suppose a liberated, independent woman like yourself would find a man's protection completely abhorrent."

He made her sound like a shrew, and she resented it, especially since he was absolutely right. She put some physical distance between them by walking back to the tape recorder.

"I have never wanted or needed a man to protect

me," Tamara insisted, refusing to look at him. "I'm not the least bit interested in changing my independent status."

"I'm not talking about radical changes," Rane argued. "I'm suggesting a ceremony that makes you my legal wife. That should be enough to make Tralosa back off." The black look swept across his features again. "He won't threaten me or anyone related to me by marriage."

He sounded arrogantly sure of that. Tamara didn't doubt he was right, but she wasn't even positive that Tralosa was responsible for the attempts on her life.

"Your name might be protection against one madman, but think of the social and legal hassles we'd face with that sort of arrangement. Think of the press and endless questions. Why bother? Besides, Tralosa might not be involved at all. Someone else might be trying to hurt me."

Rane nodded, realizing she hadn't given him an outright refusal. She was considering all the angles. He wanted to investigate one particular angle. "Are you worried about Skip Reardon? Are you still pining for him or hoping to patch up your differences? You seemed concerned about his reaction."

Tamara didn't want to discuss Skip, but she would, just this once. "I think of my relationship with Skip as a personal failure that wounded my pride, not my heart," she confessed. "I wanted out of the relationship and he made it difficult, but I have no desire to punish or humiliate him."

Good. Rane had hoped she was free of emotional involvement. Judging by her tone, she'd never been too involved with Skip in the first place.

"So there's really nothing and nobody to keep you

from marrying for convenience," he persisted, his eyes piercing.

"Only common sense and keen survival instincts," Tamara taunted, turning from his intense scrutiny. She slipped on the recorder to hear the rest of Katie's taped message.

Rane knew when to advance and when to retreat. The subject was far from closed, but he could be patient as long as he had Tamara by his side.

"Our telephone has been ringing off the hook!" Katie continued in excitement, making Tamara cringe. "Everybody wants to hear the details and I don't even know them myself!" she wailed, making Tamara feel like a heel.

"Aunt Lucinda is a little upset with you. She was really looking forward to a major-big wedding. Both of us are totally disgusted at not being in on the secret. Uncle Harold isn't saying much, at least not to me, but Aunt Lucinda has been reading him the riot act. She thinks he knew and didn't tell."

Tamara flipped the button again and turned on Rane. "This is not going to work! I can't have them believing I deliberately deceived them. I have no reason to hurt Katie and Aunt Lucinda. What kind of values am I instilling in Katie? How do you think I'll feel if she follows my example and elopes with the first boy she thinks she loves?"

"You don't have to lie to Katie or anyone else," Rane countered calmly. "Katie and Lucinda can be told the truth. They won't be upset once they know the deception was necessary to protect you."

"You don't think they'll question the morality of me spending an entire month alone with a man I hardly know?" Tamara wondered.

"They don't have to know where we spend that time. For all they know, we could be in the Bahamas, surrounded by chaperons."

Tamara cringed. She'd planned to go to the Bahamas on her aborted honeymoon. She wasn't about to tell them where she really was, yet she wouldn't lie to her family.

"You don't have to give them details," Rane continued. "Katie will be happier thinking she's part of a conspiracy. Just tell them we can't divulge confidential information."

Rane had a good point, but Tamara still glared at him before switching the recorder to the on position. She didn't want to think about all the repercussions of such a deceitful scheme. She wanted to hear her sister's voice.

SEVEN

"Seriously, Tamara, I'm really happy for you. I didn't want to say anything to hurt your feelings, but I never wanted you to marry Skip. I was so afraid you were going to make up with him and get married."

Tamara's eyes widened in surprise. Katie had never even hinted at objections to her marriage.

"I was afraid if I complained too much you might think I was jealous of Skip or that I was totally selfish. I really do want you to be happy, but I knew you didn't love Skip the way a woman should love the man she marries."

Tamara's eyes clouded and she shook her head in resignation. Katie was a hopeless romantic. She thought the world revolved around star-crossed love.

"Now, Rane Masters is a whole 'nother ball game," Katie drawled suggestively, making Tamara flinch and Rane chuckle. "He is one cool dude and a totally awesome hunk."

Rane roared with laughter and Tamara flipped off the

machine again. She tried to look stern and disapproving, but Rane's laughter was contagious. A smile curved her lips.

"It's not that funny," she admonished when he continued to laugh.

"I think it is," he said with a chuckle. "You wanted to make sure Katie was all right. I'd say she's in rare form. Besides, she thinks I'm a totally awesome hunk."

"Katie's always in rare form, and before your head swells too much, I want you to know she also thinks Doogie Houser is an awesome hunk."

Rane laughed again, and Tamara tried to ignore the pleasure she experienced at the sound. She turned back to the recorder and listened to Katie.

"So when are you and my new brother-in-law coming home? I've always wanted a big brother, you know, and I already like Rane." Katie's childlike enthusiasm made Tamara wince, wondering if she'd somehow failed her sister. There was so much wistfulness in Katie's tone that Tamara wondered if she had smothered the other girl with protectiveness. Katie had never developed close bonds with anyone but family. Tamara switched off the recorder.

"It's really not fair to deceive Katie," she spouted. "I've never lied to her and I don't want to start now."

Rane was fascinated by the mixture of emotions playing across Tamara's features. Katie obviously tapped a deep well of emotion within her. He found himself wondering what it would be like to generate so much devotion.

"You don't have to lie," said Rane. "You can tell her the truth when we get home. Right now, just let her believe we're married. It's for her protection as well as yours.''

Tamara grudgingly accepted the fact that he might be right. A touch of the button brought Katie's youthful voice back into the room.

''I suppose you know that Rane has a zillion friends. Mr. Andrews, the man who is delivering this tape, has three sons and one of them is going to be guarding the house around the clock. Uncle Harold said he didn't think it was necessary, but Mr. Andrews says he's following Rane's orders.

''It's all right to call him Rane, isn't it? Mr. Masters sounds pretty formal for a brother. I had no idea the two of you were in love! You certainly fooled us! Do you think he'll like having a sister? Could you tell him hello for me? Anyway . . .''

Katie updated Tamara on her visit with Aaron Connors and her high hopes for learning some special dives. Then she said that Uncle Harold and Aunt Lucy wanted to say a few words.

Harold pretended ignorance of the abduction fiasco and even went to so far as to congratulate the two of them. He told Tamara not to worry about a thing while she was gone and to enjoy an extended vacation.

Lucinda scolded, congratulated, and then repeated Harold's assurances that everything would be fine while she was gone. Just before the tape ran out, Katie's voice came on again.

''Tammy Jo!'' she exclaimed in sudden consternation. ''Don't you dare let Rane hear this. He'll think I'm a nerd!''

''Don't you dare think she's a nerd,'' Tamara insisted in a light tone.

''I think she's a sweetheart,'' was Rane's reply. ''I

also think you've done a great job raising her, Tammy Jo.'' He tacked on the nickname to capture her full attention.

"Repeat that nickname and I'll strangle you with my bare hands," she replied. "How soon can we get a tape back to them?"

This tape had been air-dropped from a helicopter, but someone would have to land to collect Tamara's taped response.

"Dave will land tomorrow to pick up your response. Then we'll repeat the process once a week."

Tamara sat down in an easy chair and looked as though a weight had been lifted from her shoulders. Rane had known Katie was important to her, but he was learning just how important.

"Am I allowed to send a message to Katie?" he asked, grinning.

"Why are you smiling like that?" She wanted to know. "And what are you planning to tell Katie?"

"Just that I'll take care of her sister and my men will take care of her. That shouldn't cause any problems, should it?"

Tamara eyed him speculatively. Rane Masters was full of surprises. Normally, she had men sized up, analyzed, and categorized in a matter of hours. Masters just didn't seem to fit any of the standard molds.

"Are you planning to censure what I say to her?" Tamara asked him.

"You'll just have to be careful," he replied. "I know you don't want to lie to her, but she'll be safer if she goes on believing her misconceptions. When she learns the whole truth, she'll understand the situation."

"You heard what she said about having a brother,"

Tamara reminded. "I don't want her hurt or disappointed. She's at a really sensitive age."

"She's a bright, spirited young lady, Tamara," he said. "She's capable of accepting the situation without being hurt."

"She's still a vulnerable young girl and I can tell she's hoping for a strong relationship with you."

"And you want to make sure that doesn't happen?" Rane asked tersely.

Tamara was surprised by his flair of temper. Did he want a teenage girl worshipping him? "The two of you might never have time to become well acquainted."

"In other words," he clipped, "you intend to make sure Katie and I don't get a chance to know each other better."

"Do you really want to know her better?"

Rane was thoughtful for a minute. He knew his answer was important to Tamara and any relationship they might share. "I never had a brother or sister," he declared. "I think Katie is a good kid. I'd like to get to know her, even if it's not in the brotherly fashion she's expecting."

His words surprised Tamara. He obviously intended to become closer to her family, not fade into the background when they returned home. Her pulse accelerated at the thought.

"I only want to insure that Katie doesn't get hurt."

"I won't do anything to hurt her," Rane promised. "I've experienced your anger and I don't know if I can survive another onslaught of your temper."

"My temper?" spouted Tamara.

"You did knock me down and try to pound me into the ground," Rane teased, his eyes wicked.

"Only after being mightily provoked!" Tamara defended, blushing and jumping to her feet. At the time she'd acted on instinct, but remembering the way they'd wrestled on the ground made her hot with embarrassment.

Rane loved to see the color in her cheeks and was glad that thoughts of their physical contact caused such a reaction. He wondered what she thought of the night they'd actually slept together. He'd slept on the couch last night. Looking at her was enough of a temptation, lying beside her would be dangerous. His longings hadn't diminished, but he was being careful not to initiate any unnecessary contact.

"So we're going to send a joint tape," Tamara declared, quickly changing the subject. "What am I supposed to say if I can't tell her the truth?"

"You could always ask questions about what she's doing or let her act as go-between for you and your store staff."

"She'd like that, I imagine," Tamara conceded. "But what are you going to say to her?"

"I think I'll tell her about my ranch and my mother," Rane said, watching Tamara closely for reaction. He'd known Harold's nieces for a good while, but they'd never shared much personal information.

Although she wouldn't admit it, Tamara was wildly curious about his private life. She didn't want him to read her reaction in her eyes, so she turned her back to him and began to reset the tape recorder.

"Why don't you start and then I'll finish when you run out of things to say. If there are any personal items you'd like to have sent, just tell Katie and they can be delivered with the next drop."

Tamara was amazed to realize that she couldn't think of a thing she needed. She could use a few heavy night-gowns, but she'd very quickly become attached to the flannel shirt Rane had loaned her. During the time since their agreement to coexist, she hadn't wanted for anything.

Together, they composed a taped message for Tamara's family. She was careful to keep her tone normal. She didn't comment on her supposed marriage to Rane, but discussed the fact that she would be gone a while and was enjoying her vacation.

She asked Harold and Katie to deliver messages to her assistants along with some important papers from her briefcase. But when she began to get immersed in business details, Rane very gently insisted that it was his turn to talk.

Tamara listened to his warm voice as he spoke to her family and was assaulted by a deep longing that she couldn't really define. She'd never consciously longed for a man in her life or for someone to share her responsibilities, but she had hoped that any man she cared for would understand her devotion to her family.

Life at the mountain cabin settled into a fairly peaceful routine for the next week. Rane and Tamara kept themselves occupied without spending a great deal of time together. Tamara took on the cleaning and cooking chores without complaint. She actually enjoyed homemaking tasks and found comfort and pleasure in the simple chores she performed.

When she wasn't busy working about the cabin, she took advantage of the well-stocked bookshelves and lost herself amidst the best-sellers. She had many of the same publications at home, but never seemed to find the time to read them. Whether working or relaxing, Tamara took full advantage of Rane's stereo system and kept the cabin filled with music.

Except for the first aborted attempts at escape, she never left the cabin. Rane spent most of his days outdoors; chopping wood, making repairs on the property, or fishing.

At first, Rane assumed that Tamara's aversion to the outdoors was directly related to his being there. Then he began to realize that she felt more secure in the modern confines of the cabin. He couldn't help but wonder at her behavior.

She'd moved through the forest with the natural instincts of a mountain-born creature, yet now she didn't even come outside for a breath of fresh air. He found himself wanting to coax the more natural aspects of her character into full realization, but he bided his time for a while.

Two weeks after the arrival at his hideaway, Rane decided it was time to alter their newly-formed habits. They'd become friendly companions on an impersonal level. They'd argued about politics, the arts, and even business methods. They'd nurtured a healthy respect for one another's viewpoints, but had cautiously avoided any probing into each other's private thoughts and feelings.

Rane wanted more. He knew he was playing with fire, yet his desire to get to know Tamara more intimately increased every day. His physical desire for her had increased, too, but he found his need to win her trust was more important.

The next hot, sunny afternoon, Rane sauntered into the cabin and leaned against the counter where Tamara was frosting a cake she'd baked.

"Wanna go swimming?" he invited, his eyes daring.

"In a mountain stream?" Tamara quirked a brow at

him. "Do I look like I was born yesterday?" she drawled in a discouraging tone.

Rane's features took on a devilish grin. "The thermometer is reading about eighty degrees," he informed while his senses absorbed the sight and scent of her.

"Then go dip your thermometer in that icy stream," she shot back. "Mountain water comes from mountain peaks of snow and it never gets warm enough to suit me."

She couldn't help but smile when Rane threw back his head and roared with laughter. She liked the sound very much and she was continually amazed at how easily they teased one another.

Since he rarely dressed in anything but cut-off jeans, she couldn't help but like the looks of him, too. He had a gorgeous body, all solid muscles and bronzed skin, stretched in a big, lean, sensually appealing form. There had been too many times when she'd wanted to reach out and touch him, but the thought always made her feel uncomfortably wanton. Especially since he'd honored his promise not to touch her first.

"Okay, so it's a little chilly," Rane conceded with a chuckle. He dipped his finger in the her bowl of frosting and grinned wickedly as he tasted the confection.

He was challenging her on a personal level. Tamara was surprised. He'd been annoyingly well-behaved for so long that she'd stopped being on the defensive all the time.

Now, the devilish gleam in his eyes sent a ripple of sensual shock from her head to her toes. As always, when he was near, her pulse began to beat in a pagan rhythm.

"I'm sure it's shockingly frigid," corrected Tamara as she tidied the kitchen. She argued for the sake of arguing, but she couldn't contain the wild excitement that filled her. Rane had obviously decided to destroy a few of his self-imposed barriers between them. The idea both thrilled and frightened her.

"All right," he conceded, "we'll postpone the swimming, but how about a little fishing expedition?"

Tamara was annoyed at how fiercely her heart began to pound. Rane wanted her to go outdoors with him. Her eyes locked with his as she considered the possible consequences.

The cabin was safe, it was her haven. As long as she remained indoors, she was surrounded by sophisticated reminders of her contemporary life-style. Inside, she wasn't faced with reminders of their isolated location.

She wasn't afraid of the forest. But if she spent much time outdoors, the heavy atmosphere of the wilderness seeped into her very soul, suffocating her. She would be accosted by memories of her childhood home and all the old fears would rear their ugly heads.

Tamara knew Rane couldn't understand her wariness. She had tried to escape through the forest that first night, but her frantic desire for freedom had outweighed the emotional trauma.

She wasn't sure how she would cope if the memories overwhelmed her. She didn't want him to realize how much of a coward she really was.

"Do we have to eat what we catch?" she stalled. Her desire to be with him was overshadowing her doubts.

"Not if we don't catch anything." His tone was light, but he sensed something was wrong. From her expressive features, he could tell she was battling deep emotions.

"What kind of bait will we use?"

"Fat, juicy worms," came his teasing reply. His

heart began to pound painfully. She was going to trust him.

"I won't bait the hook," she warned, noting the flare of pleasure her tentative acceptance brought to his eyes. She didn't dwell on her own delight at pleasing him.

"Every fisherman has to bait his own hook," Rane continued to tease, afraid to move too quickly and shatter the fragile faith she'd placed in him.

"Well, I'm a fisherwoman and my daddy always baited the hook for me," she replied and then her mouth remained open in shock. It was the first time she'd spontaneously referred to her father in more than ten years.

"Did he?" Rane queried softly, not wanting to upset her. He wondered if her father was at the root of her emotional insecurity and fears.

"Do you have a spare fishing pole?" Tamara asked, turning from Rane's watchful eyes and finishing her small cleaning chore.

"I have several. I'll even let you have first choice," he offered gallantly.

"How far do we have to go?" She was going with him, but she still had some serious doubts.

"The stream is about sixty yards from the back door."

Tamara glanced at the familiar scene beyond the porch. For at least twenty yards there was a grassy clearing and then the forest seemed to threaten. She had to face her fears and put childish insecurities behind her. It was a simple solution. The sun was shining and they weren't likely to get stranded or lost. Rane would be with her.

"I guess I should get a little fresh air and sunshine," she said as she brushed flour from her cotton shirt, then wiped her hands over her denim shorts. "Katie will expect me to have a glorious tan."

Rane watched her nervous gestures and wondered about the source of her tension. He wanted to snatch her close to him and hold her until all her fears were crushed. He'd begun to think of Tamara as his woman— however primitive that might seem—and he ached to know what had caused the painful insecurities his intelligent, independent lady-friend harbored.

"Come on, I'll show you where I keep my fishing gear," he told her, reaching for her hand.

Tamara looked at his big hand for an instant and then grasped hold of it. She immediately felt some of the tension subsiding. His hand was strong and warm, exciting, yet comforting as he pulled her through the back door and toward the shed where he kept his fishing tackle.

She remained calm as they moved about the clearing that surrounded the cabin, but when they stepped beneath the canopy of trees that marked the forest line, she grew tense again.

Rane sensed her distress as soon as they plunged into the darkly-shadowed foliage and he placed a bracing hand at the base of her spine. He spread his fingers and flexed them in a supportive fashion, then quickly guided her to another clearing, next to a wide, shallow stream that ran through his property.

"See, that wasn't so bad, was it?" he whispered close to her ear.

The husky tenor of his voice soothed her, tempting her to turn into his arms and cling to him. Instead, she tried to lighten her mood with small talk.

"Is this where you come to fish?"

"This is where I caught the bass we had last week,"

he told her, setting down his tackle and bait boxes. "Hold your pole while I bait the hook."

"If I catch anything, I'm going to throw it back in the water," Tamara warned him as he set about the task of baiting both their hooks.

"Uh huh," Rane replied, seemingly unconcerned by her declaration.

With a slow, fluid flick of her wrist, she expertly cast the line into the still water.

Rane's brows rose and he glanced at her in genuine surprise. "You seem more than a little proficient at this."

"Wanna argue about it?" she queried testily.

Rane grinned and shook his head. She would explain when she was ready, but not a minute sooner. "Nope," he replied, then cast his own line in the water.

"Do you fish often?" he had to ask.

"Nope." Her succinct reply was accompanied by a sassy grin.

Rane's answering smile was slow, warm, and incredibly sexy. Tamara caught her breath and quickly shifted her eyes toward the stream. The man was a constant threat to her composure, but she did love his company.

Tamara eased herself down to the ground and sat Indian fashion on the thick grass. She turned her face up to the sun and basked in its warmth, luxuriating in the warming rays. Surprisingly, the beauty and tranquility of the surroundings eased her tension.

While Tamara was relaxing, Rane also sat down and propped his pole on a makeshift stand. Then he leaned back on his forearms and watched Tamara. The sunlight brought out golden highlights in her hair and he felt an urge to release the thick mass from its braid.

If he could have his every wish, he would undo all

the buttons on her blouse and maybe even help her discard it altogether. Her long, shapely legs were nicely exposed by her shorts, yet Rane wouldn't have minded tossing them aside, either. She was too incredibly lovely to keep wrapped in clothes.

For two long, agonizing weeks he'd been tormented by memories of her exquisite body. His senses came alive every time she was within yards of him. He'd spent many restless nights remembering her responsive reactions to his tentative lovemaking.

What would it be like to love her without restraint? He closed his eyes and felt a tremor course through him at just the thought. They would be so good together. She had the capacity to match his passion with an intensity that he could only dream about and ache for. He had promised not to push her, yet he hadn't promised not to touch.

For once, Rane ignored all the mental warnings. He reached out a hand and placed it possessively on Tamara's thigh, his fingers gently kneading her silky flesh. He felt her muscle tighten in reaction to his touch, but she didn't slap his hand or shove it from her leg. Their eyes met; his dark and hungry, hers startled and wary.

It was a mistake to look into the velvet darkness of his eyes. Tamara was instantly swept into the tidal wave of his erotic emotions. Her heart began to race at the blatant need she saw there. Her flesh was on fire at his touch. Her thoughts churned with apprehension, excitement, and indecision, but this time she couldn't hide from her own emotions.

Rane recognized the confusion in her eyes, but he was encouraged by the fact that she didn't resist as he slowly eased her flat on her back. He leaned closer, propping one forearm beside her head and allowing the hand on her thigh to her shift to her midriff, beneath the blouse. He lowered his head, without losing eye contact for a second.

His hand seared her stomach like a branding iron, and Tamara thought she would always feel the mark of his touch. She couldn't seem to breathe as she watched his head block the sun and felt his warm breath whispering across her lips.

"I want a kiss, just a kiss—or two," Rane murmured as his lips brushed hers once, lightly, and then captured them with a hunger that he could no longer contain or deny.

Tamara wasn't shy about returning his kiss with all the passionate fervor he inspired. Her arms slid around his broad shoulders and her fingers kneaded the smooth flesh. He was so big and warm and virile. Her arms locked about his neck as she encouraged him to deepen the kiss, her tongue joyfully welcoming his as it plunged into the honeyed depths of her mouth.

She tasted so hot and so sweet. Suddenly, he was battling to control the hunger that raged in him. He shifted closer to envelope her with both arms and hold her tightly against his chest.

When their bodies were crushed closer together, desire—like a wildfire—rushed over Rane's body. His tongue captured and sucked hers until they both moaned in the agony of need. Rane felt a shudder rip through his body as Tamara made little mewing sounds of pleasure.

Then he was afraid. More afraid then he could ever remember being with a woman. He feared the strength of his desire, her responsiveness, and his own shattered control. He was afraid of destroying the tentative trust she'd placed in him.

Reluctantly dragging his mouth from Tamara's, Rane let her see the raging need in his eyes. Her eyes were alight with matching hunger and a low groan escaped him.

"You're so beautiful and responsive," he rasped, stealing another swift, hard kiss. "I don't want to do anything to hurt you."

Tamara was already hurting, but she didn't have the courage to tell him that. Instead, she tugged his head back down and fastened her lips on his with wild abandon. She felt him tremble and her blood ran hotter than lava. The next thing she knew, she was being lifted off the ground and carried in his arms.

"Rane?" she questioned huskily.

EIGHT

"Time to cool off," he told her gruffly, his eyes burning into hers.

It took a few seconds for his intention to sink into her passion-fogged brain. "Rane, no!" she argued uselessly as she felt him step from the bank into the stream.

"It's not too bad," he told her and kept moving until he felt the numbing cold on his loins. He closed his eyes and groaned, then eased Tamara's feet into the water.

"It's freezing!" she screamed, clinging to his shoulders as her feet touched bottom and the icy water enveloped her to the waist. "I hate it!"

Rane managed a chuckle, his humor returning as his ardor cooled. "That's sissy talk."

"This sissy won't cook your dinner or let you have any cake tonight," she warned as he held her captive, refusing to let her move back to the shore.

"If you're that much of a wimp, you can wrap your

legs around my waist and I'll hold you out of the water."

Tamara glared at him, but followed his suggestion and managed to wrap her legs around his middle, sighing with relief when most of her body cleared the cold water. She clung tightly to him with her arms around his neck and her legs wrapped about his waist. He supported her weight with both hands under her rear end and they stared at one another, eye to eye.

"You're totally insane," she accused, slightly embarrassed by the intimacy of their new embrace.

"I'm a totally awesome hunk," he reminded while tugging her closer. "I'm also a totally frustrated hunk," he drawled, watching the blush run up her cheeks. "It seems with you and me that everything either has to be hard and hot or shockingly frigid."

Tamara buried her over-heated face in the curve of his shoulder to hide from his devilishly taunting eyes. She wasn't used to such blatant sexual innuendo. She was growing accustomed to his provocative teasing, but she hated feeling like such a schoolgirl when he managed to embarrass her.

It was time to demonstrate a little sophistication and wipe that smug grin from his face. Without considering the consequences, she sunk her teeth into the tendon of his neck.

His arms immediately tightened around her and he grew rigid with tension again. She knew she'd succeeded in throwing him off balance when he shuddered and moaned in reaction.

His hot, seeking mouth scorched its way up her neck to her mouth. "If this is your idea of revenge," he whispered against her lips, "you're playing a dangerous game."

A dark, turbulent expression filled his eyes. Tamara was instantly ashamed of her deliberate teasing. Rane was trying to protect them from making a serious mistake, and she wasn't helping at all.

"We're supposed to be fishing," she insisted, holding perfectly still so that her movements wouldn't add to his discomfort. "Maybe we should get out of the water and stop scaring the fish."

Rane accepted her unspoken apology and headed for the bank, managing to splash more icy water over them before depositing her on the ground where she'd been sitting earlier.

Together, they tugged off their sopping wet tennis shoes and checked the lines of their fishing poles, making sure the bait was intact. Then they relaxed in the warm grass once more.

Tamara threw back her head and welcomed the golden rays of sunshine on her face. A little shiver raced over her as the heat of the sun began to penetrate the chill of her clothing.

"Why don't you take off your clothes," Rane suggested, turning his full attention to her again.

Tamara eyed him warily. She'd love to take off her wet clothing and let the sun's warmth engulf her, but she didn't think it was wise under the circumstances.

"I might sunbathe in the nude if you weren't here," she told him, her tone suggesting that he could leave.

"You can do whatever you like, with or without me," he countered, shifting closer to her. "I won't bother you."

He always bothered her, Tamara thought. Then she caught her breath as he reached out and slowly unfastened the buttons of her blouse. She barely dared to breathe as he finished his task and slipped the fabric off her shoulders. He thoughtfully draped the blouse over a nearby bush and turned back to her.

She could tell by the sudden narrowing of his eyes that he hadn't been prepared for a skimpy lace bra with bows, a front catch, and very little fabric covering her straining breasts.

Rane clenched his teeth as desire flashed through his body. He was determined to resist temptation and make Tamara feel completely comfortable in his presence. He took a deep breath and reached for the snap of her shorts.

"I don't think that would be a very good idea," she told him. Her voice sounded low and husky to her ears because her pulse was already beating a deafening rhythm in her head.

"Your shorts must be sticky and uncomfortable." Rane's voice was just as low and rough as hers. "Mine are."

"You're not taking yours off," she pointed out softly, maintaining eye contact.

"It's safer for mine to be cold and clammy," he explained huskily. "Besides, your underwear is as good as a bikini."

"Not really," Tamara argued. Her underwear was an extravagant leftover from dreams of a romantic honeymoon. It clung like a second skin and left little to the imagination.

Still, the heat of the sun and the equal heat in Rane's eyes made her feel bold and sensual. She unfastened her own shorts and wiggled out of them.

Her skin was like honey; golden and sweetly enticing. Rane's pulse pounded in his ears as he watched her stretch out on the thick carpet of grass. He turned on his side toward her, determined to protect her from his passion, yet unable to completely resist temptation.

Tamara started when she felt his hand splay on her stomach. Her eyes darted to his, questioningly.

"I want to touch you," he explained in a soothing tone.

"You told me not to play games," she replied breathlessly. His touch always seemed to steal her breath.

"I'll be all right as long as you don't touch me."

"That's not quite fair, is it?"

"Probably not," he conceded, watching his own fingers as they skimmed the lacy curve of her bra. Tamara's chest was heaving in sensual agitation and Rane was totally fascinated by the rhythmic rise and fall of her breasts.

His fingers slowly inched their way to her rigid nipples. Tamara closed her eyes and forced herself to swallow the moan of pleasure she felt when he continued to caress first one turgid peak and then the other.

His touch was so light and teasing that it created an ache deep in the core of her, making her want much more than he was offering.

"Rane!" she pleaded, not even sure what she wanted or expected of him.

In response, he unclipped the front of her bra. Then she felt the heat of him as he leaned closer and took a throbbing nipple into his mouth, suckling gently.

Tamara's hands were balled into tight fists and her toes were curling even tighter. Rane felt her tension and tasted her excitement. He knew he was creating an ache every bit as painful as his own, but he loved touching her.

She felt like satin and tasted like woman. He didn't

want to leave her aching, but he didn't know how she'd react if he tried to satisfy her without risking intercourse. He didn't want to alienate her altogether, so he tried to soothe her with a slow withdrawal of his caresses.

Tamara was half-irritated, half-relieved when Rane's touch became less intimate. She forced herself to breathe slowly and deeply until she'd stilled her own rampaging desire. Then she dared to lift her eyelids.

A strong volt of emotion passed through them as Rane stared directly into her eyes. "I told you you were a dangerous man," she managed on a shaky sigh.

"Because you like me more than you want to?" he asked roughly. "Because I make you feel like a desirable woman? Because you've never wanted to make love to any man the way you want to make love to me?"

Tamara's lashes swept down to conceal her reaction to his questions. Yes, she liked him too much. Yes, he made her feel vibrantly alive and utterly feminine. Yes, she wanted him more than any man she'd ever known.

But what did he really want? An affair? Just a satisfying physical relationship? Perhaps she could accept his offerings if he only wanted physical release, but she had a gut feeling that Rane Masters would never settle for a mutually-independent relationship. He was one of those "all or nothing" kind of guys. She couldn't give anyone her all or she'd have nothing left.

"Talk to me," Rane commanded gently. "Tell me what you're thinking."

Tamara didn't know how to discuss such private wants and needs. Instead, she depended on teasing banter to distract him. "I was thinking that if somebody would leave me alone, I might be able to take a nap in the sun.''

"Is somebody bothering you?" He feigned innocence, but drew his hands back to his sides.

Tamara heaved a gentle sigh of relief when Rane withdrew his touch. He threatened her composure and made her feel wild and wanton. She wasn't sure she liked losing control or being totally uninhibited. She did enjoy the unique freedom from embarrassment and modesty. She also enjoyed the pagan pleasure of the sun on her bare flesh and didn't hurry to cover herself.

"Talk to me, Tamara," Rane reiterated. He stretched out on his back, closed his eyes and tucked his hands safely under his head.

"What would you like to talk about?" she stalled. She knew by the tone of his voice that he wanted serious talk, not teasing repartee.

"Tell me about yourself. Tell me how you can navigate in these mountains like a wild creature and later shudder in revulsion when you have to leave the security of the cabin.''

Rane's sensitivity to her irrational hang-ups was both warming and alarming. He made her want to explain herself and she'd never wanted to do that before. She knew she could trust him with the truth and she found herself sharing her most intimate secrets.

"I was born and raised in the mountains," she told him quietly. "Not these mountains," she continued. "I don't know where we are . . .''

"The Ozarks," Rane supplied without hesitation.

Tamara felt an unexpected thrill at his concession of faith.

"There are noticeable differences in the foliage and wildlife, but the mountains are the mountains.''

"Where were you raised?"

"In Pocahontas County, West Virginia," Tamara said on a sigh of regret. "The population ten years ago consisted of one family to every twenty or so miles. Besides, we lived high in the mountains and so deep in the forest that other families never wanted to be close." Her family had been truly isolated from what most people would consider normal society.

"Harold mentioned that your father was a mountain man." Rane urged her to supply more details.

"When he was twenty he decided he wanted to see the Pacific Ocean. He hired on with a pipeline company and worked his way to Texas, where he met my mother. They were married and he took her home to West Virginia."

"Did he still have family there?"

"His mother and only sister were dead. Mama said his father was still living when she first moved to the mountains, but my paternal grandfather died before I was born.

"My father was a true mountain man in every sense of the word," she explained, tugging at the grass with restless fingers. "Once he'd found my mother, he was content to spend the rest of his life at his mountain home." Tamara knew that her tone was growing increasingly bitter, but she couldn't control the wave of emotion that came with the memories.

"Were you very poor?" Rane asked, trying to understand her bitterness and wondering if an impoverished childhood was responsible for her emotional distress.

"Is that why you were afraid to go in the cabin that first night?" he asked. He propped himself on an elbow and studied the haunting loveliness of her features.

"When I look back, I realize that we were very poor

in a monetary sense,'' she explained, pulling the sides of her bra together and fastening it. The action was representative of other aspects in her life that she felt a need to conceal.

"I don't imagine my father had as much money in his lifetime as I make in one month, and that's not an exaggeration. Money just wasn't important to him.''

"How did you get by?"

When Rane leaned closer, his head blocked the sun and Tamara was able to look directly at him. "My father was poor, but far from lazy,'' she explained. "He worked hard, usually from daylight 'til dark. We had shelter, food, and clothing. He hunted, fished, trapped, and traded the hides for supplies we couldn't raise or make ourselves.

"Mama always had a garden in the summer and canned much of our food. Microwaves and dishwashers were unheard of. We didn't even have running water. Mama had a wood stove and a ground cellar, so she managed to do everything the old-fashioned way.''

"The hard way,'' Rane suggested softly, his eyes scanning her expressive features.

"Yes, it was hard,'' Tamara agreed, lowering her lashes. "But Mama always behaved like a southern lady. She insisted that I learn the rules of etiquette right along with my reading, writing, and arithmetic. We had a set of encyclopedias and she collected textbooks until she had enough to insure my basic education. She made me study several hours each day, year 'round.''

"No summer vacation, huh?" Rane teased.

"I never knew school vacations existed until I moved to Texas. Mama was worse than a drill sergeant when it came to education. My father's mother had been the same, so Mama had Daddy's support and encouragement.''

"Did your dad teach you to hunt and fish, too?"

Tamara nodded, continuing to play with the clumps of grass at her side. Rane knew that discussing her past made her nervous, but he still hadn't learned anything that might have caused her fears and insecurity.

"I was always being taught something," Tamara admitted with a grin. "Life in the mountains is hard and only knowledge and understanding of the environment can help one survive. My parents raised a survivor."

"A lonely survivor? You never left the mountains or visited with neighbors?" Rane asked. Then he placed one of his big hands over her fidgeting fingers and silently urged Tamara to hold on to him for comfort.

She clasped his hand in both of hers and rested it on her stomach, feeling warm and secure when clinging to him.

"Daddy would make two trips a year to an old general store where he traded his hides for supplies. He'd go in the spring and again in the fall. Sometimes Mama and I went with him. We had a few distant neighbors and there was a midwife who actually came to our cabin, but mostly we kept to ourselves."

"What about county officials? Didn't you get mail or get visited by government workers of some kind? How could you exist without having to account to someone?" Rane asked, wondering how any family could remain so isolated.

"My father never filed a tax form in his life. We didn't even have an address or postal number. As far as the county or government was concerned, we didn't exist, and that's the way my father wanted it."

Rane thought her dad might have been a very wise man, but he didn't think Tamara would appreciate that viewpoint.

"Was Katie your only sibling?" His brows creased in a frown when pain briefly darkened her eyes.

"For the first thirteen years of my life, I was an only child," Tamara explained, giving him a smile that dispelled the distress. "My world revolved around my parents and my pets. When Katie was born, I thought I'd died and gone to heaven. She was so little and sweet and cuddly. I was getting too old for dolls, so I smothered her with attention. My daddy used to swear I would wear her out if I didn't stop holding her so much."

"Does Katie have any memory of your parents?"

"No," Tamara responded, some of the lightness leaving her voice. "She remembers a little about our trip to Texas, but nothing before that." She personally thought it a blessing that Katie had no memories to haunt her.

"Despite the isolation and old-fashioned methods, your upbringing sounds pretty normal," Rane dared to suggest, still seeking a reason for the mental torment he knew she suffered.

Tamara's grip on his hand tightened and she closed her eyes while the memories washed over her. Being in the mountains stirred emotions that she'd forgotten. She was surprised to realize that there were good memories as well as bad.

Her father had been a big man with a strong, athletic body. She could remember him carrying her on his shoulders, teaching her to swim and fish and even how to jump rope. He would often pick her mother up and carry her in his arms. Her mother had laughed a lot when Tamara was younger. She couldn't remember either of her parents ever raising their voice to her.

Tamara opened her eyes and smiled at Rane. "You're right. Over the years I've blocked out a lot of the good memories by refusing to face the bad ones. I never doubted that my parents adored Katie and me. We were loved and nurtured like children should be. I was taught how to work, to play, and to accept responsibility."

"But?" Rane encouraged, shifting closer to her side.

"But there were bad times, too."

"Too bad to talk about?" he inquired softly.

Tamara was lulled by the sun, the lazy day and Rane's presence. "My parents were normal, healthy adults. They loved each other and they didn't believe in birth control. My mother had two miscarriages before I was born, five between me and Katie, and two after Katie. I watched her grow increasingly weak and fragile, but she wouldn't consider leaving the mountains and seeking medical attention. She wanted to give my father a son."

"And your father?"

"I don't know how he felt about it. All I know is that he didn't take her to a doctor and she kept getting pregnant."

"And you blame your father for that?" Rane asked, realizing that they were finally getting near the root of her fears. He didn't want her to clam up on him now, so he tread softly. "It takes two to make a baby," he put in gently, squeezing her fingers with his own.

Tamara ignored the subtle suggestion of responsibility. "My mother got weaker with each pregnancy. It took her months to regain her strength after Katie was born. I don't think she ever really recovered from the next miscarriage. Then my father was killed in an accident while she was carrying the last baby and when she miscarried, she just gave up and died.''

Rane wanted to pull Tamara into his arms and hold her. He wanted to help her mourn the loss of a father, a mother, unborn siblings, and her own emotional security. Losing so much in so short a time had left her with permanent scars.

His arms ached to comfort her, but he sensed that she needed some measure of distance between them. Tamara couldn't help but compare her experiences from the past to their present situation. He was responsible for isolating her, yet he hoped she understood that their circumstances were very different.

''When we first arrived here, you thought I knew about your past, didn't you?''

Tamara looked him directly in the eyes and then shifted her gaze. ''At first I thought only the devil could know my past. I've never discussed it with another living soul.''

''And our wrestling match that first day?'' Rane inquired lightly. ''You were panicked at the sight of a cabin as rustic and isolated as you'd grown up in?''

''At first,'' Tamara conceded. ''I wasn't thinking too clearly, just feeling very confused and vulnerable.''

''I want you to know that I have never and would never do anything to deliberately hurt you,'' Rane told her, his tone demanding that she believe him. ''I brought you here because I love this place and because it has always had a healing effect on me. I had no idea that it would affect you in the opposite way.''

Tamara was warmed by his concern and she believed him. She pulled herself into a sitting position and brought his hand to her lips, brushing a soft kiss across his knuckles. ''I think your hideaway could have a healing effect on me, too," she told him. "I've lived with the insecurities for a long time, but you've helped me remember some of the good things.

"I'd forgotten the unique sounds, the taste of mountain water, and the clear, brilliant colors. There's a peace and harmony here that's been missing from my life for a long time."

Rane understood. He gently withdrew his hand from her grasp and handed her blouse to her. "You'd better put this back on before you get too much sun," he said, sitting up and wrapping his arms around his knees to keep from wrapping them around Tamara. This time, he might not let go.

"I still don't understand why your fear of the mountain is so intense," Rane questioned without looking at her.

Tamara buttoned her blouse and wondered if she could explain all the horror that she'd felt that last winter in West Virginia. The extremes—bitter cold and blinding bright outside, darkness and suffocating heat inside, the isolation, the fear.

It was easier to talk to Rane's back while he busied himself with his fishing pole. "My birthday is in September and I'd just celebrated my seventeenth when Daddy made his fall trip to get supplies. I didn't go with him because Mama was pregnant and we didn't want to leave her and Katie alone," she recalled, reliving those last days with her family intact.

"September was a beautiful month, but October turned harsh and cold. Daddy was chopping down a small tree to stock firewood for the winter and something went wrong; a freak accident or change of wind brought the tree down on him. We were never sure what happened, only that his skull was crushed and he was dead. Mother and I buried him in a small family cemetery.''

Rane's hands clenched on the fishing pole until it threatened to snap. His heart ached for the pregnant wife and sensitive young girl who'd had to deal with such a brutal shock.

Tamara absently checked her shorts and turned them in the sun so that they would continue to dry. Her thoughts were absorbed in the past.

''We considered moving closer to civilization when Daddy died, but Mother wasn't capable of traveling twenty miles on foot or by mule. Since we had plenty of winter supplies, we decided to wait until spring before we moved. The baby would have been born by then, so we thought it best to stay at home.''

Tamara went silent as she relived the horror of the last dark winter confined to the cabin for the biggest part of every day, seven days a week. She hadn't dared to leave her mother or Katie alone and neither of them were able to stay outdoors very long. Tamara could feel the numbing cold and constant fear she'd lived with for months after her father's death.

''My mother lost the will to live,'' she stated baldly. ''She grieved herself to death and she had another miscarriage. I begged her not to leave me, but nothing I could do or say seemed to matter,'' Tamara declared in a strangely detached tone.

''She told me that she loved me and repeatedly explained that I was to take Katie to Texas, but she didn't want to live.''

Rane turned to Tamara, gathering her in his arms. She might not need the comfort, but at this point, he needed it. She stayed rigid in his arms, but she didn't pull away from him.

"You must have felt abandoned and scared to death. How long were you alone?" he asked, his mouth pressed against her ear as he began to gently rock her in his arms.

"Mother died in January," Tamara continued in a dull tone. "The ground was too frozen to bury her, but I couldn't keep her in the cabin, so I had to keep packing her in snow until the ground thawed."

Rane closed his eyes and made soft, comforting sounds in Tamara's ear as he continued to rock her. He imagined the terror of a teenager being so totally alone. Most adults would have lost their minds trying to deal with the grief and she'd had to deal with a corpse and a preschooler. How had she coped, physically or mentally?

He could understand her initial panic when he'd brought her to his cabin and had tried to force her inside. He had unwittingly opened a Pandora's box of agonizing memories.

The last images of her dead mother were burned into Tamara's memory: the cold, lifeless, frozen features. Then there was the emotional and physical burden of the actual burial once the ground was soft enough.

"Thank God you had Katie," Rane whispered.

Tamara's arms slipped about his waist and she rubbed her head against the breadth of his chest. "Katie was my sanity," she explained. "Without her, I think I might have given up and died with them."

Rane made an angry sound and Tamara actually smiled.

"Katie became my security blanket. My parents had insured that we had the necessities to survive physically, but Katie kept me from losing my mind that winter."

"And in the spring, you buried your mother and brought Katie off the mountain," Rane supplied for her.

"It was the longest winter of my life and the most difficult spring, but I thought I had put it all behind me."

"Then along came Masters and brought back all the pain," Rane growled in self-disgust.

Tamara eased out of his arms and gave him a smile, but her eyes were still haunted. "You didn't know. Maybe it was meant to be. Maybe I needed a reminder of all the good that came before the bad. I guess I've been selfish by denying the good memories for so long."

"Why selfish?"

"I should have shared the special times with Katie and Harold and Lucinda. I've never told them how much Daddy and Mama loved one another and how happy we were together."

"You have good reason for not dredging up the past," Rane injected gruffly, feeling stunned by the details of her battle for survival. Katie had helped her maintain her sanity. He owed that little lady a debt of gratitude.

NINE

Tamara moved a little further from Rane and reached for her shorts. They were almost dry, so she wiggled into them. When she felt less exposed, she rose and walked to the edge of the water. Her thoughts were whirling with scenes from the past, scenes that she'd refused to remember for so many years.

Her mother and father had been beautiful people, inside and out. They were devoted to each other and to her. If they'd ever yearned for a life beyond the mountains, they'd hidden it well. Life had been harsh, but filled with laughter and love. Her mother's declining health was the only thing that dampened their enthusiasm for the life they shared. The idea of repeating her mother's mistake was a deep-seeded fear of Tamara's.

"What made you decide to change your name to Bennington?" Rane broke the growing silence with his question.

Tamara turned to him, a bit surprised at the reminder that her legal name was not her father's. "Daddy's name was Crackens, but Uncle Harold wanted to legally adopt us and I had no objection. When I first went to Texas, I wanted to destroy all ties with the past. The Bible I carried with me was the only record of births and deaths for my whole family,'' she tacked on derisively.

"Your father didn't have any living relatives?''

"No,'' Tamara was sure of that. "Mountain living is a harsh life.''

"Not for us,'' Rane insisted, grabbing one of her hands and tugging until she sat beside him again. "We're on vacation.''

Tamara laughed with him, feeling free and light-hearted. She was beginning to believe that Rane Masters was the best thing that had ever happened to her. Unfortunately, that knowledge brought an innate fear with it.

"We haven't caught one fish for dinner,'' she told him, nudging his pole with her bare toe. "I'll bet the bait's long gone and the hook is stuck in the mud.''

Rane ignored her comment and concentrated on the long, smooth length of her legs. His expression was so pointedly lecherous that Tamara began to giggle.

"Behave yourself or I might not feed you at all tonight,'' she warned as she playfully smacked him on the shoulder.

Rane laughed and grabbed her hand, tugging quickly and tumbling her against his chest. He wrapped both arms around her and squeezed her briefly, then laid down and tucked her close to his side.

Tamara nestled her head near his shoulder and let one hand rest on his stomach as she relaxed again in the sunshine.

Rane closed his eyes and sighed with pleasure. He

was content with their progress toward a sharing relationship and more than pleased by Tamara's willingness to trust him.

"Comfortable?" he asked her.

"Uh huh," she replied, idly running her fingers through the swirling hair on his chest.

"Find anything you like?" he taunted.

Tamara was emboldened by his affectionate teasing. "I don't have any soft, curly hair on my chest," she complained.

Rane spared her an admonishing glance, then closed his eyes again. "You can play with mine any time you like."

Tamara laughed at his solemn declaration and gave him a spontaneous hug. Then her hand relaxed on his stomach again.

"It seems like I've been doing all the talking this afternoon," she noted absently. "Are you willing to answer some questions for me?"

She felt Rane grow tense and was surprised that her casual request might bother him. "What's the matter, Masters?" she teased. "You weren't the least bit hesitant about bombarding me with questions."

"What do you want to know, Tammy Jo?" The lightness of his tone belied the tension in his big body.

If he thought he could distract her by using her silly nickname, he had another think coming. She was insatiably curious about him and she'd had two weeks to formulate a wealth of personal questions she wanted answered.

"You could start by telling me about these strange scars on your stomach," she told him, running her fingers over the cluster of scar tissue. "Did you have chicken pox and scratch when your mother told you not to?''

Rane lifted a hand to cover hers. He never thought about them anymore. The small circular scars were barely noticeable unless someone got really close.

Tamara wondered at his delay in answering. She wished she could recall the question, especially if he was sensitive about the marks. She was curious, but only because he never wore a shirt. The faded scars were an intriguing imperfection on an absolutely gorgeous male body.

"Do you find them repulsive?" he asked quite seriously.

She found them utterly fascinating, just like all the rest of him, but she didn't say so. Instead, she leaned over and planted a kiss across the scarred area.

The moist heat of her mouth momentarily froze Rane, then caused a resulting shudder to rip through his body.

"Damn, Tamara, don't do things like that," he rasped, grabbing a handful of hair and pulling her head level with his.

Her eyes were alight with curiosity and admiration. His wore an expression of excitement mingled with frustration.

"You don't like it?" she breathed softly.

"I like it too damned much," he countered roughly.

"So do I," she admitted lightly. "So how dare you imagine that I find anything about you repulsive?"

Rane heaved a sigh, grinned derisively and relaxed, shifting her to the curve of his shoulder again.

"Some women get spastic about scars or deformity of any kind," he explained. "I've never had any complaints, but there's always a first time,'' he added wickedly.

Tamara pinched him hard, but otherwise ignored the mention of other women, even though the thought made her momentarily see red.

"I'm waiting," she declared softly, letting him know that she wasn't going to be distracted from her original question.

Rane didn't want to discuss that particular part of his background. He knew Tamara's respect for him was growing and he didn't want to remind her that he was an ex-convict. Still, he didn't suppose there would be any better time to answer her questions. He wanted an honest, open relationship.

"I told you I was in a Mexican prison," he finally managed, his voice low. "I wasn't a very cooperative inmate and the guards used various ways to punish me for misbehaving."

"They tortured you?" Tamara gasped, rising from her relaxed position to stare at him. Her hand went to his stomach and gently caressed the scarred area. "How could they do such a thing!"

Some of the tension left Rane's body and he chuckled at her indignation. "They do what they damned well please and they chose to use my stomach for an ash tray."

"They deliberately burned you?" Her heart filled with compassion for the proud, but frightened teenager he must have been. The fingers on his stomach trembled and she turned so pale that Rane immediately regretted telling her the truth.

"It was a lifetime ago," he soothed in a gentle tone. "At the time, the pain was a welcome reminder that I hadn't lost my fighting spirit."

Tamara continued to stroke the old scars with gentle fingers. "Tralosa was responsible for this," she growled. "I hope he rots in prison. Then burns in hell!"

"Me, too," Rane agreed, laughing and enjoying her spirited defense of him. He drew her down beside him and made her lie still again, tucked in his arm.

"Tell me about it," Tamara encouraged.

"There's not much to tell," Rane insisted. "I stayed in prison two years and then came home to rebuild my business."

"Didn't you lose your pilot's license or anything like that?"

"The Mexican government confiscated our aircraft and that caused the business to go bankrupt. My dad tried to fight for my release through the courts, but he didn't have enough clout or financial backing."

"And he died trying to free you. I'm sorry," Tamara told him softly.

"Yeah," Rane countered with bitterness, "so am I."

They were quiet for a few minutes. Tamara knew that Rane was lost in memories, just as she had been. She wanted him to share with her, but wasn't sure about asking.

"How long a prison term were you given?" she tentatively queried.

Rane's disgusted grunt didn't sound much like the laugh he'd intended. "The Mexican government would have kept me indefinitely," he said. "They weren't about to give back that plane without compensation."

"How did your mother manage to raise the money?"

Her question targeted the most traumatic aspect of Rane's release from that hellhole. He'd never discussed it, even with his mother. He wasn't sure how to explain.

"There was a wealthy rancher who idolized my mother. He knew she was devoted to my father and had no desire to remarry after his death, but he made a bargain with her," Rane explained, the bitter truth causing bile to rise in his throat.

Tamara didn't want him to go on. She could feel the coiled tension in his body and hear the tortured guilt in his tone. "It doesn't matter," she tried to convince him.

"It doesn't matter that my mother prostituted herself to get me out of prison?" he argued, pushing himself away from her and running a rough hand through his hair. Then he was on his feet.

"She married him, then used his money and influence to get the charges against me dropped. My record was wiped clean and my plane returned. All it cost my mother was her soul."

"You sound like you condemn her for helping you."

"No! Never!" Rane swore, glaring at her. "I'd have sold my own soul to get out of that prison."

"But you wouldn't have sold your mother's?"

"No."

"Do you think she's continued to suffer over her decision?" Tamara asked lightly, feeling that Rane needed to talk about the guilt he carried.

"No," Rane had to admit. "Mom seems to take everything in stride. I think he treated her like a queen and maybe he never insisted on consummating the marriage, I don't know. He died a few months after I was released. He might have known he was dying when he married Mom. I just never had the guts to ask her."

"And she never brought up the subject? Maybe she

thinks you lost respect for her because she married for money.''

"That's crazy! She did it for me!" Rane insisted, grabbing his pole and reeling in the line. "I've never been able to find the right words to tell her how much I appreciate what she did for me. Except for my first few days of freedom when I was recuperating, we haven't discussed the subject."

Rane's face was grim as he continued to gather up their fishing gear. Tamara assumed that he'd decided it was time to go, but she couldn't squelch her curiosity.

"Do you think your mother secretly harbors a resentment toward you?"

Tamara touched on the heart of Rane's concern. He hadn't been aware of how much he despised the thought of his mother's resentment or the possibility that he'd lost her respect. He knew she loved him, she'd proven her love, but after all these years, he still wasn't sure that she had forgiven him.

"How could she not?" Rane snapped. "My arrogance cost her the husband she loved and forced her to marry a man she didn't love."

"Nobody forced her to do anything," Tamara commented as she followed Rane back through the forest toward the cabin. She was so wrapped up in his problems, she temporarily forgot her dread of the darkness.

"I suppose not," Rane conceded. "My mother's a hard person to analyze. I don't really know how she feels about the whole episode and resulting circumstances."

"I know how she feels." Tamara's declaration was firm, making Rane turn and stare at her questioningly.

"Do you?" he mocked, his eyes taunting her in disbelief. "You've never met my mother, but you think you know how she feels about me?"

They had arrived at the clearing around the cabin and Rane stored their fishing tackle in the shed. Tamara waited until he was finished to make her point.

"I know how she feels," she repeated, locking gazes with him and letting him see how annoyed she was by his flippant disbelief. "If you want to know, I'll tell you."

Rane stared into her eyes and realized she was dead serious. "So, please tell me."

"Your mother feels the same way I would feel if Katie was ever threatened. It's a gripping sort of love that makes a woman capable of performing extraordinary feats. I would do anything to protect Katie from harm. Anything," she reiterated, hands on hips, eyes challenging. "But no matter what I chose to do, I'd still respect her and I'd never stop loving her.

"Your mother might think you detest the choices she made, but I'm willing to bet her respect for you has increased over the years, not diminished. She probably loves you more each day and believes your freedom was worth any price she paid."

Rane felt a tumult of emotions while he listened to her confident description of love. Part of him imagined that she might be right and that he'd wasted a lot of years worrying about his fragile relationship with his mother.

Tamara had an immense capacity to love and he envied anyone she loved. He'd never wanted a woman to be totally devoted to him, yet he was realizing that his feelings for Tamara were very different.

"You might be right," he conceded in a quieted tone.

Tamara grinned. "Of course, I'm right," she teased. "When it comes to maternal love, I'm wise beyond my years."

With that, she turned and ran toward the cabin. Rane admired her swinging backside, but his thoughts were geared toward her arguments. She had suffered greatly, yet she'd never considered relinquishing responsibility for her sister. He knew that Harold and Lucinda would have been thrilled to raise Katie. Yet Harold insisted that Tamara had always provided the maternal care and guidance. That kind of love, loyalty, and devotion was hard to come by. It was a priceless gift.

His mother had given him such a gift. But without Tamara's insight, he might never have considered the situation from a mother's point of view. When he got home, he would make sure his mom knew how much he loved and respected her; that the sacrifices she'd made only deepened those feelings.

In the meantime, he only had two weeks left to capture the heart of a very elusive lady. He was making progress, but he needed more patience. He also needed to keep a tighter rein on the desire that threatened to overwhelm him.

The next two weeks were a time of discovery for both Tamara and Rane. They no longer went their separate ways and Tamara didn't confine herself to the cabin. For the first time in her adult life, she laughed wholeheartedly, played in the sunshine, and flirted with a man in a perfectly natural fashion.

Rane didn't fight the urge to touch her. He loved running his hands through her silky hair. He loved stroking the rose-petal softness of her cheeks. He loved just holding her hand. They became intimate friends, but on a fairly platonic basis.

On Thursday of their last week at the mountain hideaway, Tamara accompanied Rane to the heliport to pick up their final tape from Katie. She always looked forward to hearing from her sister, but this day her thoughts were filled with the contentment Rane had brought to her life.

He'd helped her banish her irrational fear of isolation. She felt as though a heavy burden had been lifted from her heart, and now she actually dreaded leaving the mountain because doing so would mean being separated from Rane.

On the way back down the ridge from the helicopter pad, Rane decided they should do some exploring and take a different route than they normally used. Tamara teased him about needing a constant challenge, but she followed him with an equal amount of curiosity and enthusiasm.

Halfway to the cabin, Rane halted abruptly and stepped in front of Tamara, blocking her view of the area ahead of them.

She propped her hands on her hips and flashed him a questioning look, but could tell right away that he'd seen something he didn't want her to see.

"What are you hiding?" she wanted to know, trying to gently shove him aside.

"It's a young doe," Rane explained, his tone heavy. "It looks like she's dead. Why don't you backtrack to the cabin while I see if there's anything I can do."

"Maybe I can help," Tamara insisted. If he wanted to bury the deer, he could use some assistance.

"Tamara," he warned on a groan, not wanting her to witness the scene.

"I'm not a baby, Rane," she chided. "You can't protect me from everything sad or unpleasant."

Rane knew she was right, but he was pretty sure the doe had died while giving birth. The situation might upset her more than she realized. He didn't want to subject her to painful reminders of her past.

"Rane?"

He stepped aside, but followed closely while Tamara approached the dead animal. The scene was more disturbing than he'd expected. The doe looked very young had died trying to give birth to a breach baby. The strain had obviously been more than the small animal could survive.

Tamara's heart began to pound heavily in her chest and her throat went dry. She swallowed hard, telling herself that she shouldn't let the unexpected sight of the deer bother her. She understood the laws of survival, yet she was still appalled by the grimness of the scene.

Flashbacks of pain, suffering, and stillborn babies erupted in her mind. No amount of rationalization could alter the affect the memories had on her vulnerable emotions.

Why hadn't she taken Rane's advice and gone back to the cabin without argument? Why did she continue to consider herself tough and independent when the sight of this little family made her heart constrict with pain?

"Tamara?" There was deep concern in Rane's tone when he spoke to her. He reached out a hand and gently laid it on her arm. "There's nothing we can do."

He could see the distress in her eyes and he felt the tension in her body. He was especially worried about the sudden pallor of her skin.

"I know we can't help now, but I would feel better if you'd bury them to protect them from the vultures,"

Tamara responded quietly, turning away from the deer. She didn't make an offer to help.

Her acceptance of the situation relieved Rane somewhat, but the dullness of her eyes and distant attitude alarmed him.

"Why don't we go back to the cabin," he suggested, folding her into his arms. "We'll listen to Katie's news and I'll come back later to take care of this little family."

Tamara rubbed her cheek against the solid width of his chest and wrapped her arms around his waist. When Rane gently tugged on her hair, she tilted her head up. His eyes were as dark and concerned as hers.

"I can't bear for anything to hurt you," he admitted. "You're so compassionate that you open yourself to hurt."

"I've tried long and hard to be tough," she confessed raggedly. "But sometimes the smallest things tear me apart."

It was the most revealing statement Tamara had ever made to another person and she felt more vulnerable at the admission.

His mouth came slowly down to hers, offering comfort with the warmth of his lips brushing gently across her trembling ones. Her arms tightened to thank him for his support and understanding.

Rane suggested that they return to the cabin and Tamara nodded in agreement, following his lead, but never looking back at the deer they'd left behind. She reminded herself that it was important to look forward, not backward. What you left behind had a way of haunting you if you let it.

The remainder of the day passed quietly. Tamara was more reserved than usual, but Rane didn't try to cheer her. He knew she was suffering a lot of conflicting emotions.

She was still troubled over her past and probably worrying about the future. He wanted her to share her concerns with him, but he couldn't demand it. All he could do was wait.

Tamara didn't intentionally shut Rane out, but the scene in the woods had triggered memories too painful to express and too poignant to put out of her mind. It seemed like fate was mocking her with reminders of lessons she'd learned the hard way.

She went to bed early, with troubled thoughts that soon became troubled dreams. Her mother's image, swollen with child, was incredibly vivid. Pain, suffering, and so much blood. She could hear her mother's moans, feel the scalding heat of fever, taste the salt of her own tears.

Sweat broke over Tamara's body as she became fully entangled in the memories. She relived the last torturous days of her mother's life; another stillborn sibling, the look of total defeat on her mother's features; her own frantic voice begging her mother to survive.

Her mother hadn't wanted to live. Her will to live had died with the only man she'd ever loved. The passionate intensity of that love had ultimately cost Tamara her mother's life.

Then her own life had become a black hole where she'd been trapped in desolation. Her mother's eyes had died and her flesh had grown cold and dark and hard. Insanity had threatened, and the vivid memories caused shudders to rip through Tamara's body.

TEN

Rane didn't attempt to go to sleep that night. He shed his clothes and stretched out on the sofa, but his thoughts were turbulent. His concern for Tamara kept mounting. When her soft moans reached his ears, he leapt to his feet and strode to the bed. He recognized the struggle she was having with her nightmares. Her expression was tortured, her body glistening with perspiration.

He hesitated to wake her until she began to twist restlessly and fight the bed clothing, murmuring incoherently. He couldn't distinguish her words, but he couldn't withstand the anguished timbre of her pleas.

In one fluid movement, he slid across the bed and took Tamara in his arms, trying to quiet her desperate thrashing. She fought the unknown demons until Rane spoke to her.

"Tamara, wake up, stop fighting me," he commanded.

Her eyes opened, but they were glazed with pain and he knew she wasn't completely awake.

"I can't breathe!" she gasped, tugging at the collar of her night shirt. The buttons were loose, but she seemed to panic at the slightest restriction.

Rane ignored her flaying arms and dragged her into his embrace. Then he lifted her from the bed and carried her through the cabin to the glass-enclosed porch. Moonlight bathed the room and he sat down on the cushioned glider, holding Tamara on his lap until she came more fully awake.

His flannel shirt clung damply to her body and her hair was wildly disheveled. He could feel the mad racing of her heart. But after a few minutes of his reassuring whispers, she began to calm down.

"Rane?" she murmured finally, reaching out a hand to touch the stubble-roughened texture of his cheek.

He breathed easier when he heard the calm recognition in her voice. He was badly shaken by her distress. He was no stranger to nightmares, yet experiencing them with Tamara was the worst trauma he could remember suffering in recent years.

"It's all right, darling," he told her quietly, using the endearment for the first time in his life and meaning it with all his heart. "You had a bad dream, but I've got you now and I won't let go. Everything will be okay."

"The baby died and then Mama died, too."

She tried to explain her panic, but her words were jumbled.

Rane's heart constricted painfully, thinking that she was still upset about the deer and that it was his fault she saw them in the first place.

"There was nothing we could do." He didn't want her to think he'd been callous and uncaring. "You know that, don't you?"

"Not the deer, Rane," she told him in a distant tone.

He pulled her closer, realizing that she was talking about her own mother. He couldn't let her withdraw from him or he might not be able to get her back.

"Talk to me, Tammy," he coaxed. "Tell me about the dream. Tell me why you hurt. I want to understand and make it better."

Tamara's eyes were wide and unblinking as they stared into his. She let her head fall to the curve of his shoulder and wrapped her arms about him. Then she confided her deepest fears.

"My mother and father loved one another with an intensity that I could never quite understand," she told him, closing her eyes and letting the steady thud of Rane's heart comfort her.

"I can hardly remember a time when my mother wasn't pregnant. She carried most of the babies full term, but something always went wrong at the end. The babies were always stillborn, and Mama's labor was always so hard."

Rane rocked her and his heart ached for the sensitive child she'd been.

"I used to pray that my dad would find some way to protect her from more pregnancies. Eventually, I began to resent him for her declining health. Then I grew to hate the love that bound them together; especially when it cost my mother her life."

Rane's arms tightened and he buried his face in the softness of her hair. "You can't blame their love for all the pain and disillusion." He hesitated. "That love brought them years of happiness and gave them both you and Katie."

Tamara rubbed her cheek against the tight curls on his chest, but didn't comment. She knew that the incident with the deer had triggered her nightmares, but it was the knowledge of her own insecurities that she found hard to describe.

She was falling passionately, hopelessly in love with Rane. The strength of those feelings scared her to death. She tried to make him understand how deep-rooted her fears of loving really were.

"I loved my parents and they professed to love one another, but could a man really love a woman and still allow his passion to take precedence over her very life? My father's love of his home and his desire for physical satisfaction seemed more important to him than my mother's life."

Rane didn't like the concept of love she was revealing. He tried to make her understand that her father's love for his mate couldn't be blamed for all the heartache she'd suffered.

"Your mother must have shared his feelings. If not, she probably knew her family in Texas would welcome her home."

"I understand that she loved him, too," Tamara conceded. "I know she desperately wanted each child she carried and that she was totally devoted to my father. But all her love, loyalty, and passion ever won her was more sickness, pain, and death. Her love weakened her and finally cost us her life. I will never bear a child and I don't want that kind of love!"

The impassioned words sent a shaft of fear through Rane. Now he understood why Tamara was so reluctant to give away her heart. He understood why she'd never allowed herself uninhibited loving. In a few words, she'd condemned the things he most wanted to share with her; her love, loyalty, and passion.

He thanked God that he'd been able to control his

desire up to now. An unwanted pregnancy would surely destroy any feelings she had for him. He badly wanted to express the depths of his own feelings, yet the only way he knew how to show his love was to make love to her. If he lost control, she'd never forgive him.

"Is this a brush-off?" he asked lightly, but seriously. "Are you trying to warn me that I'd better not demand too much?" His big hand cupped her chin and tilted her head upward until their eyes locked. "Do you want me to pretend that I don't want to make love to you? That I don't want our relationship to be passionately strong and last a lifetime?"

Shifting in his lap until her breasts were crushed against him, Tamara let both of her arms slide over his broad chest and lock about his neck. She recognized the deep concern in his eyes. Her own eyes were clouded and her tone, husky.

"I'm trying to tell you that I'm falling hopelessly in love with you, but it scares the hell out of me," she whispered. "I'm trying to be sophisticated, mature, and rational, but I'm still frightened and confused."

Rane groaned low in his throat and held her closer. "I don't want you to be afraid of loving me," he rasped, his mouth descending to the softly parted invitation of hers. "I want to teach you all the sweet, positive aspects of love. I want you to trust me completely."

Their mouths locked and their tongues mated frantically; each straining to get closer to the other. All the confusion, frustration, and pent-up emotions surfaced with their passion and soon the need for one another superseded all else. Their desire could no longer be denied. They needed physical expression of their growing love.

Rane wanted to carry Tamara to bed and spend the

night making love to her until she was convinced that what they shared was special and worth a few risks. Still, his conscience wouldn't allow him to completely forget the promise he'd made or her innate fear of pregnancy.

He stretched out his long length on the cushioned glider and shifted their weight until Tamara was lying fully on top of him. His hands began to stroke her spine and his legs tangled intimately with hers.

His mouth explored the honeyed sweetness of hers until their breathing became ragged and labored. Then he allowed his lips the freedom of scattering kisses along her cheek, to her ear and to the throbbing pulse at her neck. Her hair tumbled over his face in a silken web of intimacy that made his body ache with a desire too hot and intense to be dampened.

Tamara felt her breasts being crushed against his chest, the nipples taut and aching. She wanted to feel his bare skin. Shifting slightly, she unfastened the top buttons of the shirt and slipped it off her shoulders. They moaned in unison when the rigid peaks of her breasts tangled with the tight curls on his chest.

The small act of trust on her part made Rane's body react explosively. His pulse pounded in his ears with a deafening force. His hands slipped to her narrow waist and lifted her upward so that he could slowly, but hungrily suckle each nipple while Tamara clutched at his hair with clawing fingers.

He wetly caressed first one and then the other pebble-hard peak, adoring them with teeth and tongue until Tamara's moans grew desperate and her hips began to undulate against him with increasing urgency.

Her restless actions nearly drove him out of his mind. The blood pumping through his veins was liquid fire, scorching him. He forced himself to concentrate on arousing Tamara.

He wanted her to need him more than she'd ever imagined it possible to need a man, because he wanted her more desperately than he could find the words to express.

"Rane!" Tamara finally gasped her amazement at the desire he was igniting in her. Her limbs were going weak and her blood pumped through her body at an alarming rate. The feel of his hot mouth tugging on her breast created an ache in the very core of her being.

"Your skin is so soft, your nipples so hard," Rane declared gruffly, burying his face between her breasts and enjoying the voluptuous feel of her flesh. Then he flicked his tongue over each nipple again and began a foray of damp kisses that spread over her throat to her neck and ears.

Tamara's fingers clenched and unclenched in his hair while she planted hard little kisses across his forehead. She continued to wiggle against him so that the solid width of his chest would soothe the ache in her nipples. She was aching all over and couldn't stop the involuntary begging for closer contact. She knew she was losing control, but Rane's heat and hunger fueled the flames of desire.

His hands slipped beneath the flannel shirt and slid the fabric over the curve of her hips. He intended to slide it off her body completely, but when his hands encountered the silk-covered curve of her hips, his fingers clenched, pulling her even closer to the swollen hardness of his groin. His hips lunged upward to grind against the cradle of her thighs.

Their mingled moans were low and tortured. Tamara kicked off her nightshirt and rubbed against the pulsing hardness of Rane's nearly nude body. Their flesh glistened with dampness as moonlight bathed them with sparkling brilliance.

Their lips locked to convey the primitive urgency. Tamara's hands slid boldly to Rane's hips, trying to rid him of his briefs. He swiftly dodged her attempts by turning on his side and effectively trapping her between the back of the glider and his massive body.

He secured her arms around his shoulders. His lips left hers and roved again to her pouting nipples; his continuous adoration driving her to a fever pitch of excitement.

With one arm about her body, he used his other hand to begin a sensual assault on the supple skin of her belly and then the juncture of her thighs. Tamara gasped at the feel of his calloused fingers on her most tender flesh, but her body very rapidly let him know that she liked the new sensations he was creating. Low, hungry sounds escaped her throat while the rest of her body rocked against Rane's in insistent demand.

Tamara's fingernails dug into the muscles of his shoulders while her hips and legs thrashed in restless longing. She felt the rock-hard evidence of Rane's arousal, but his caresses soon drove all other thoughts from her mind. Nothing mattered but that he relieve the tension escalating to an unbearable level in her body.

"Please, Rane!" she begged. "I want you so badly!" came her ragged admission of need.

Tremor after tremor coursed over Rane's body as he fought to harden himself to her pleas. He was dangerously close to exploding. He ground his hips into hers, swallowing her panting breaths while he turned her more fully onto her back and began to caress her with renewed fervor.

His fingers and the palm of his hand rhythmically stroked her until she began to rotate her hips in a feverish attempt to match the fervor of his caresses. "Rane! Oh, Rane!" she cried as the tension built to an unbearable level. "No!"

"Don't fight me, Baby," he begged, his voice raw. "Let me make it good for you."

Tamara cried out again, her head thrashing from side to side until Rane captured her mouth and swallowed her cries of release and satisfaction. Her body convulsed against his in violent reaction. Her chest rose and fell in agitated breathing while her legs reflexively locked about his thighs.

Rane's breathing was tortured, his body throbbing with need, but he enjoyed bringing her satisfaction more than he'd ever enjoyed anything in his life. He wanted to bury himself deep within her, but now he was really afraid of the strength of his own need. He didn't want to hurt or frighten her.

He continued to caress and kiss Tamara until her breathing became less labored. His big hands stroked her trembling body until she relaxed and reopened her eyes.

"Rane?" she managed throatily, wanting to know why he'd been so determined to satisfy her and not himself.

"I promised, remember? And I'm not a monster. I want you, but not at any risk," he answered huskily.

Tamara loved him more at that minute than she'd ever thought it possible to love a man. A sob rose in her throat and she hugged him fiercely.

"I do love you!" she swore, her eyes filling with tears as her heart overflowed with emotion.

"And I love you," Rane confessed just as huskily. "But I won't force you to accept my love."

Tamara gazed at him with eyes that were blurred with tears. She tried to hold him tighter, but when her body brushed against his, she was made more aware of his state of arousal. Her eyes pleaded for guidance.

"How can I make it better?" she whispered softly.

Rane's smile was warm and adoring. He knew she really wanted to give him satisfaction and he ached so badly that he didn't even consider denying her or himself.

"Touch me," he rasped, knowing that her lightest touch would be his undoing. "Just touch me."

Tamara swiftly complied with his gruff urgings. She slid a hand beneath the straining elastic of his briefs and enveloped the satin-smooth hardness of his flesh. His moan was long and low, his need swiftly satisfied.

Later, when their bodies had cooled and calmed, Rane carried Tamara to bed and held her close. There was no way he could let her out of his arms tonight, although he knew the contentment would be short-lived. Their loving had been really special, but he didn't trust himself to indulge in that sort of lovemaking again. His desire for Tamara burned too high and he wanted to be a part of her, locked together with a pledge for a lifetime of loving.

"I think it's about time we head home," he whispered into Tamara's ear as he buried his face in the silky softness of her hair. "Harold said Tralosa's trial will go to jury tomorrow. It will be safe soon."

Tamara shifted her head so that she could look directly into his eyes. She knew him too well to fret about his not wanting to spend more time alone with her.

"We're not expected back for a few more days."

"We can stay here until we get an all-clear from Harold, but the sooner we face the real world and come to terms with our relationship, the better," Rane insisted.

She wasn't sure she shared his philosophy. The outside world was bound to complicate their relationship. They both had major responsibilities; totally unrelated and incompatible responsibilities.

"You think we'll be better off if we go our separate ways?" she asked, wanting to know just where she stood with him.

"Hell, no," Rane growled, "but I can't handle much more of this pretending that tomorrow doesn't exist. We need to make some decisions about a future. I want to marry you."

Tamara's whole body stiffened and her eyes widened with shock. Rane resented her reaction. They'd both just confessed their love, didn't that mean anything? Was the idea of getting married to him totally unthinkable for her?

"I don't know why the suggestion comes as such a surprise," he insisted, his tone growing cool. "We discussed the idea when we first learned that all of San Antonio thinks we eloped."

Tamara's breathing was shallow. When he'd asked her to get married, her heart had completely stopped. She'd thought he was serious, but now she realized he was just making the suggestion to protect her when they returned to Texas.

"You really think that a wedding ceremony would eliminate problems instead of creating more?" she asked.

Rane didn't want her believing that his proposal was strictly for propriety's sake. But he wanted her to agree, regardless of her reasoning.

"We could fly to Las Vegas before returning to Texas. Being married would eliminate a lot of awkward explanations and possibly ward off any further attempts on your life. I know Tralosa would think twice before threatening my wife."

Tamara was perversely relieved and annoyed by his reasoning. If she and Rane were to marry, she wanted it to be a marriage based on love. On the other hand, she felt panicky and reluctant to trust her own judgment on the subject of everlasting love.

She couldn't bear the thought of being parted from him. Still, she couldn't handle a marriage of convenience. She would spend the rest of her life wondering whether Rane really wanted her as a wife. He might say he loved her now, but how would he feel once they were home again?

"No, not this way," she protested lightly, her eyes beseeching him to understand. "After one disastrous engagement, I can't make that kind of decision on the spur of the moment."

"Spur of the moment?" Rane challenged, hating the distance she was already putting between them.

"It just wouldn't be right," Tamara insisted, turning on her side with her back to him.

She had a valid point, even if Rane didn't like it. A Las Vegas marriage wasn't exactly her style. He wished she were eager and willing to marry him for any reason, but that wasn't the case.

He tightened his arms around her and drew her close to the warmth of his body. Then he heard Tamara's soft sigh.

"Good night, Rane," she murmured.

"Good night."

ELEVEN

Early the next morning, Rane went to the helicopter and radioed Dave Andrews for news from Harold. He learned that Dave had been frantically trying to reach him. There was trouble at home and they needed to return immediately.

Within an hour, Rane was flying Tamara off the mountain. They landed the helicopter in St. Louis and transferred their belongings to his jet. Then he flew them across country toward Texas.

Tamara believed they were going home because Harold had declared it safe. Rane didn't want her to know the whole truth until they neared San Antonio. He didn't want her worrying unnecessarily.

For most of the flight, Tamara rested. The emotional stress of the previous day had left her exhausted, so she slept in the cabin. When she woke, she was refreshed and alert.

Rane welcomed her into the cockpit with a smile. "Hello, sleepyhead," he teased, then softened his tone, "feel better?"

Returning his smile, Tamara placed a kiss on his cheek and settled into the copilot's seat. "I feel like a new woman," she told him. "Thanks for letting me sleep."

"It was hell to do without you for a few hours," he commented lightly, "but I'm tough."

"Besides," she charged, "there's not a thing I can do to help you fly this plane."

"You can keep me company," Rane supplied. "I've missed your lovely face and your charming conversation."

"You missed my non-stop chatter, you mean," Tamara continued the playful banter. "Now that I'm wide awake, you can tell me why you decided to come home today. Even if Harold thinks it's safe to return to San Antone, we didn't have to hurry. You didn't have to bundle me up and hustle me out of there before I was even awake."

Rane was quiet for a long time, wondering how to explain why he'd been so anxious to get back to Texas. He wished he could protect her from worry, but he had to tell her.

"Rane?" Tamara prompted, growing alarmed by his lack of response. "Has something happened at home? Something serious? Has someone been hurt?"

"Everyone's okay," he assured her. "There's been trouble at your uncle's ranch. Nobody was hurt, but Skip tried to abduct Katie." There was no gentle way to break that news.

"Katie!" Tamara panicked. "Is she all right now? Was she hurt? Katie must have been scared to death! If he hurt her, I'll kill him!"

Rane turned and grasped Tamara's face, planting a long, hard kiss on her lips for reassurance. Then he straightened. "Katie wasn't hurt or badly frightened. Andrews told me that Skip walked right up to the door and Katie let him in the house. She had no reason to be wary of him."

Tamara gasped. It was all her fault! She'd never had any reason to warn her family against Skip. "What did he do?"

"I guess your aunt and uncle were out back in the garden, so Skip tried to coax Katie out the front door. When she wouldn't cooperate, he used a little chloroform. Fortunately, one of Dave Andrews' sons, Don, got to them before Skip made it to the car."

"Chloroform!" Tamara screamed. "I'll kill him!" She was seething. How dare that lowlife attack her sister! What in the hell did he hope to accomplish by abducting Katie?

"Has he totally lost his mind?" she screeched.

"Harold called Lieutenant Carlile. He's been doing some investigating. It seems that Skip has a gambling problem and he's in serious debt to one Anthony Tralosa."

Tamara paled. "Oh, my God!"

"Yeah," Rane shared the sentiment. "Carlile's informant says Skip promised Tralosa he would keep you under control, but then you broke off the engagement and left Skip in a bind."

"And Skip made those attempts on my life?" she gasped, still reluctant to believe he'd wanted her dead.

"At first, he just wanted to scare you. He probably thought you'd turn to him for protection and reconsider marrying him. When you refused to scare, he got desperate."

"And when I disappeared, he went after Katie,"

Tamara concluded. "That despicable scum. I hope Carlile locked him up and threw away the keys!"

Rane's expression tightened. "Unfortunately, Carlile doesn't have Skip in custody. Don was more concerned about protecting Katie than apprehending Skip. Skip got away and they haven't been able to locate him."

Tamara ran a trembling hand through her hair. "So Skip knows he's in deep trouble now and he's liable to go to any extreme," she surmised grimly. "When did all of this happen?"

"Last night," Rane told her. "Andrews tried to radio us, but we weren't near the helicopter. He told me this morning. He's got five of my best men watching Harold's ranch. I don't think Skip will risk going out there again."

"How long will it take us to reach San Antonio?"

"Another hour."

Rane glanced at Tamara and smiled slightly when he realized that she was still muttering threats. "You should really be glad that Skip used a little chloroform. Katie might have been hurt if she'd tried to fight him. Instead, she slept while Don Andrews kept her safe."

"But what in the world did Tralosa hope to accomplish by having Skip kidnap Katie? Her abduction could only cause him bad press. It would do more harm than good."

"Tralosa didn't plan the abduction. When he heard the rumor that you and I had married, he told Skip to stay away from you."

That's exactly how Rane had supposed Tralosa would react, thought Tamara. The gangster obviously had more sense than Skip.

"So Skip is acting on his own behalf now."

"He had an entirely different reaction to the

rumors," Rane supplied. "He's out for revenge now. The spurned lover, it would seem."

"Skip was never my lover," Tamara snapped irritably.

Rane's grin was wide. "I stand corrected," he said. "The jilted bridegroom."

"Right," she clipped. How had she ever become involved with Skip in the first place? Why had it taken her so long to see beneath the southern charm and laid-back attitude? Skip obviously had a dark side to his nature that she'd never even suspected. Now her family was suffering and endangered due to her poor judgment of character.

Did she dare trust her own judgment again? Did she dare risk so much of herself? Would she be risking her family's welfare and security if she trusted anyone too much? Wouldn't they all be safer if she isolated them from outside influences?

Tamara stared at the brilliant blue sky surrounding the aircraft and became lost in thought. Rane was busy navigating the jet and remained silent. The two of them began to mentally prepare for a return to their individual responsibilities.

The relaxed, leisurely pace of the past month would quickly dissipate once they were home. They braced themselves for the changes they'd be forced to undergo. Neither of them wanted to dwell on the fact that they'd eventually have to go their separate ways and tend to their business.

They were both used to heavy responsibilities. For the past month, they'd been pretending the demands on their time didn't exist, but it had been a fanciful pretense. Reality was due to hit them soon. The time had come to learn if what they'd shared in the mountains could survive the pressures of their individual worlds.

Whatever the future held, they knew they could never be happy if being together meant hurting all the people who depended on them. They had personal commitments that needed to be honored before they could make a lifetime commitment to one another.

"I think it would be wise to let everyone assume we're a happily married couple returning from our honeymoon," Rane said at one point on the flight.

Tamara nodded her agreement. She wasn't sure just how honeymooners were supposed to behave, but she wasn't prepared to go into intimate details about their relationship, either. She would have to explain everything to Harold and Lucinda, but that could wait until her family's safety was insured.

They touched down in San Antonio in the heat of the afternoon. The blistering sun was a painful reminder that the comfort of the mountains was far away now.

Tamara felt her stomach roll nauseously as she helped Rane transfer their belongings to his car. She blamed the heat for her discomfort, but she knew that the impending changes in her relationship with Rane, however slight, were making her physically ill. She hated the unrelenting emotional turmoil.

Rane started the car and had the air conditioning blowing cool air before they'd left the airport, but Tamara's stomach refused to stop churning. She realized that she was genuinely nervous and frightened. She didn't like the feeling at all.

Rane was equally worried. He didn't like the distance that was gradually developing between them. When she returned to her family, would he lose her altogether?

Tamara's heart quickened as they turned in the gates

of Harold's ranch. Rane waved to his men on guard and then pulled to a stop in the drive. Before they had climbed from the car, the front door was thrown open and Katie came flying down the drive. She threw herself into Tamara's waiting arms.

"Tammy! You're home!" she squealed as she fiercely hugged her sister. "You're really home!"

"Yes, I'm home." Tamara laughed and cried at the same time. The tears were of relief at finding Katie as exuberant as ever. "You're okay? Skip didn't hurt you?" She squeezed her sister tightly, amazed at how much she'd missed her.

"I slept through all the excitement," Katie dismissed the issue in disgust, holding Tamara at arm's length. "You sure look super. I think you've gotten more beautiful!" she exclaimed.

Tamara laughed happily. "They say absence makes the heart grow fonder. Maybe it affects the eyesight, too."

Katie giggled, but she shook her head. Tamara was different. The contentment in her sister's eyes was new. She was more tanned and relaxed than Katie had ever seen her.

In some ways, Katie was beyond her years. She turned her eyes toward Rane, knowing instinctively that he had given Tamara something that no one else was capable of giving her.

"So," she drawled softly, "did you make my sister more beautiful? Don't you know that I already have an awesome image to live up to?"

"You'll make it," he assured. Then he surprised them all by opening his arms. "Don't I get a hug and kiss?"

Katie didn't hesitate a second. She flew to his arms

and hugged him fiercely while planting a loud kiss on his cheeks.

"Welcome to the family, Rane Masters."

Harold and Lucinda reached the three of them in time to hear Katie's enthusiastic welcome. It might have been an awkward situation, but Tamara didn't want to ruin the moment for anyone or start making explanations. All the questions and answers could come later.

"Katie thinks she wants a big brother, but wait until she finds out what an awful tease this man is. If she thinks I'm bad, Rane holds the world's record for teasing," Tamara insisted, hugging her aunt and uncle tightly to convey her true feelings, while she verbally made light of the situation.

"And he doesn't think young girls should date until they're at least twenty-one," she invented as she turned back to her sister.

Katie gasped and stared at Rane with wide eyes.

"She made that up," he defended, affectionately tugging a lock of Katie's hair. "She's just trying to blame me for her old-fashioned views of child rearing."

"Old-fashioned?" Tamara argued in her own defense. "I don't have an old-fashioned bone in my body. Katie's the dyed-in-the-wool romantic of this family."

"Being romantic does not make me old-fashioned," Katie protested in one of their ongoing arguments. "Does it Rane?" she asked, looking to him as a champion of her cause.

"Not in the least," he replied smoothly, knowing he was taking sides, yet unconcerned. Tamara began to protest, but he wrapped an arm about her shoulders and planted a swift, hard kiss on her parted lips.

For just an instant, their eyes locked, and a very

fierce, very private need erupted between them. Rane stole another kiss, trying to soothe the ache of withdrawal they were already experiencing.

Harold loudly cleared his throat, his expression smug. Lucinda beamed at them and Katie stared in astonishment.

Tamera's lovely features were flushed with heat as she witnessed the reaction of her family to the intimacy between her and Rane.

"My God!" Katie exclaimed, staring at her sister as though she'd never seen her before. "Tamara's blushing," she declared dramatically. "My sister, the corporate dragon, has turned into a blushing bride! I can hardly believe my eyes!"

No one could resist Katie's clowning and they all joined in laughter, but Rane's hold on Tamara tightened. He was afraid she might be offended by the teasing.

Instead, Tamara turned laughing eyes up to him and returned his hug. "Sometimes I think I've created a monster," she said of her baby sister.

"Well! I like that!" Katie huffed. "It's not like you actually molded me from clay. I do have a mind of my own!"

"Indeed, you do." This came from Lucinda. She hugged Rane and added her welcome, but didn't bombard him with questions. "I'm so glad you're home, but you must be tired. Let's get into the house where you can relax."

"What we need is food," Tamara declared. "We've been airborne most of the day and I'm starving. I know Rane is, too."

"Well, good heavens, we can take care of that," Lucinda insisted, leading the way indoors.

After a meal was prepared and eaten, they spent a couple hours just visiting. Tamara noted that her aunt and uncle were watchful of her and Rane, but the subject of her abduction wasn't mentioned. Harold had obviously confessed his involvement to Lucinda, but nobody seemed anxious for Katie to learn the details.

Rane made phone calls to his ranch staff and the police department. The situation with Skip was discussed, yet no one was sure what to expect next.

"Lieutenant Carlile says there's a warrant out for his arrest, but Skip hasn't been near any of his regular haunts."

"Do you think Tralosa is hiding him?" Harold wondered.

"No," Rane was certain of that. "Carlile thinks Tralosa's men are trying to find Skip, too. The big boss wants to have a talk with him."

Tamara and Rane exchanged a concerned glance. It wasn't good news. If Skip had double-crossed Tralosa, there could be a contract out on him. And if Skip was being hunted by both the law and the mob, he would be desperate and very dangerous.

"I don't think Skip is fool enough to bother anyone here at the ranch," Rane reassured. "We'll keep the guards posted until he's found and jailed."

"What about my apartment?" Tamara asked. "I need to go in town and get some clothes. I want to check my messages, my mail, and make some phone calls." Harold had assured her that everything was fine at the office, but she wanted some direct communications for her own peace of mind.

"You don't have to go anywhere this evening, do you?" Rane asked.

"You're planning to go to town, aren't you?" she countered, fearing that he would leave without her.

"I have to go to the police department and talk to Carlile for a while, but it won't take long."

"Are you planning to come back here tonight?" Tamara insisted, knowing that neither of them would be completely comfortable spending the night at the ranch with her family.

"I have to stop at my apartment, and then see what Carlile has in mind," he answered without promising his return.

Tamara's eyes reminded him that this was her battle. She wasn't letting him go anywhere without her, regardless of the threat Skip posed. "I'm going with you."

Rane frowned and Harold protested, but Tamara abruptly countered their arguments. "I refuse to stay in hiding. For all we know, Skip might have left the country. I'm not going to allow him to disrupt my whole life."

Rane knew he should argue. Tamara would be safer here, but he didn't want to leave her. He wanted to spend the night making love to her, yet he didn't want to spend their first night together in Harold's home. He wanted her all to himself.

"We can take a guard with us to watch your apartment and I'll see what kind of backup Carlile can provide," he said, watching relief drain some of Tamara's tension and wondering if his selfish desire to keep her near him was a mistake.

Tamara released the breath she'd been holding. She was relieved that Rane didn't want to be parted from her any more than she wanted to have him leave. She also knew that if Skip was going to try anything insane, her family would be safer if she wasn't under the same roof.

It was early evening when they left the ranch. Tony Larson, one of Rane's big, mean-looking employees, accompanied them into San Antonio. Tamara chatted with him at Rane's apartment while Rane showered, changed clothes, and sifted through his mail. He called Carlile again and promised to come to the police station as soon as he'd gotten Tamara settled.

Next, they went to Tamara's apartment. She leased the entire second story of a modern complex that employed security guards, but Rane and Tony still wanted to check all the rooms, including every corner of the closets and under the beds.

She had a huge living room with a terrace, a dining room, kitchen, two bedrooms, and two baths. They scoured every inch of it.

Tamara switched on the air conditioning and listened to the messages on her answering machine while Rane checked the locks on the windows. Tony made sure her electric wiring and gas lines were safe. Nothing was amiss. Everything was just as it should be.

When Rane felt certain her apartment was safe, he pulled her into his arms and hugged her. "I'm going to the police department to talk to Carlile. Tony can stay with you until I get back. I promise I won't be gone more than an hour. Okay?"

Tamara slipped her arms about his waist and squeezed tightly. She felt a rush of warmth and the feeling of security she always experienced when she was close to him. She wanted more than a hug, but they weren't alone.

"I'm just going to shower and find something comfortable to wear that isn't made of denim,'' she offered lightly.

"Slipping into something a little more comfortable?'' he teased in a low tone, his eyes smiling with intimate warmth.

"You just hurry back and find out for yourself,'' she countered lightly, her eyes promising him untold delights.

Rane brushed a light kiss across her lips and reluctantly released her, turning towards the door. If he didn't leave soon, he'd never find out what Carlie knew about Skip Reardon. The lieutenant refused to give details over the phone and insisted on meeting with Rane tonight.

He turned to Tony. "Carlile promised to send an unmarked patrol car over here. If you hear anything at all, or suspect anything out of the ordinary, just flash the living room lights three times and ring for the security guards.''

Tony nodded in agreement. Tamara thought all the precaution unnecessary, but she was pleased by Rane's concern.

"Don't be gone long,'' she told him.

"Lock the door behind me and let Tony take care of any phone calls or unexpected visitors.''

"Yes, sir,'' was her sassy response.

Rane grinned. Then he was gone.

Tamara felt bereft the instant he was out of sight, but she berated herself for such silliness. She couldn't keep him by her side forever. She needed to revive her independent spirit.

"Tony, can I get you something to drink? I don't think there's much food in the apartment, but their should be some soft drinks in the fridge.''

The big man looked out of place amongst the blue, cream, and lavender pastels in her living room.

"You don't have to worry about me, Mrs. Masters," he returned politely, sitting down on the velvet sofa.

"Well, make yourself at home," she insisted. "I need to take a shower and get rid of some of the dust I collected today."

"Yes, ma'am," he returned. "I'll just sit here in the living room and make sure nobody bothers you."

"Thank you, Tony." Tamara knew he was loyal and dependable or Rane wouldn't have him here, but he looked like a fish out of water. Rane's men were employed to run a ranch. They weren't trained body-guards. Still, he was big and strong enough to deter any intruder. "Excuse me while I go shower."

Tony nodded and Tamara went into her bedroom. The decor was an extension of the pastels, in soft hues of blue and green, and enveloped her with a feeling of well-being.

She chose a pair of satin lounging pajamas to wear. They were sky blue and made her feel like a femme fatale when she wore them. They had elastic at the waist and above her breasts, but no buttons or zippers. Rane should love them, she mused with a grin.

After laying the pajamas across her bed, she shed her dirty clothes and moved into the bathroom where she showered and washed her hair. When she was dry again, she spent more than half-an-hour styling her hair, letting it hang loose over her shoulders in heavy waves. She applied some makeup to highlight her eyes and lips. Then she slipped into the satin pajamas and dabbed a touch of perfume at pulse points.

Excitement coursed through her at the thought of the night to come. Memories of Rane's incredible blend of tenderness and passion made her ache in a way she'd never experienced.

Tamara wanted this night to be so special. She wanted to express her love in the most elemental fashion, to be be all the woman Rane could ever want or need. She wasn't experienced in a sophisticated fashion, but her love was so strong and her desire so intense, she no longer worried about disappointing him.

Tamara tidied her bedroom and bath, then dimmed the lights before returning to the living room. She came to an abrupt halt at the doorway when she saw Skip standing over Tony's inert body.

Her first thought was that he'd killed the other man. "What have you done!" she charged, automatically moving closer to the unconscious man on the sofa.

Skip's eyes flared in maniacal delight as she moved closer and Tamara abruptly halted her advance.

"I just used a little chloroform on the big guy," Skip told her flippantly, discarding a chloroform-soaked handkerchief on Tony's prone body. "It works every time," he added maliciously, deliberately reminding her of his attack on Katie.

White-hot anger gripped Tamara and caution was tossed to the wind. "That's your style, isn't it, Skip?" she hissed at him. "You're good at slithering around and sneaking up on defenseless people, aren't you? You're especially adept at attacking children and unsuspecting women," she added in a scathing tone.

"Do you ever face an adversary on equal footing? Do you possess one ounce of real strength or courage?"

"Shut-up, bitch," Skip commanded, moving menacingly closer to her.

Her contempt had obviously enraged him. He'd probably planned to do all the taunting and take command of the situation, but Tamara wasn't behaving the way he'd expected her to. She wasn't cowering or frightened or submissive.

"How did you get in here?" she demanded, refusing to back down, but mentally preparing for flight should he get too close.

"Through Katie's bedroom," he boasted. "I just cut out a little section of window glass, then reached in and unlocked the window." He raised his hand to show Tamara the sharp blade on the cutter he still held in his hand.

The sight of the weapon caused her to catch her breath and feel the first quivering of genuine fear. Tamara forced herself to glare directly into Skip's eyes.

"What do you want, Skip? There's no chance of a reconciliation between us and I know about Tralosa. He told you to leave me alone. What do you expect to gain by harassing me?"

"Just what's mine," he snarled, his eyes as cold as ice. He was looking at her with pure hatred.

Raised in the lap of luxury, Skip had been given everything he ever wanted. He refused to believe he couldn't have her, Tamara thought. He was an extremely attractive man with the blond good looks of an all-American male. But today the blue eyes were chilling and his handsome features haggard.

He moved closer and Tamara took a step backward. She was barefoot and the thin fabric of her pajamas left her feeling too vulnerable. She wasn't worried about defending herself against Skip, but she was very much afraid of the blade he was wielding.

"You owe me, Tamara," he said, slowly inching closer to her. "You're mine. I waited months to have you. I played the perfect gentleman while you kept me at arm's length, but I'm done playing games.

"I'm going to have what's mine. Then I'm going to fix you so that no other man will ever want you." His eyes wore the look of a madman, his voice slurred, and he waved the cutting blade at her to emphasize his intentions.

A shaft of fear raced down Tamara's spine and her heart began to pound in panic. He was insane. And she didn't doubt that he meant every word he was saying.

Where were Rane and Carlile and the security guards? She slowly backed toward her front door. The light switch was near and she remembered Rane telling Tony to flip the switch for help. If Skip weren't so close, she could ring for the security guards, but she knew he wouldn't let her get near that buzzer.

Skip's sudden burst of laughter was maniacal. "It's just you and me, Tamara. There's no place to run." He cackled as he slowly inched closer, savoring his small victory.

"Nobody's going to save you this time. Uncle Harold is at the ranch. Masters is at the police station. The security guards and police officers think you're safe and sound. It's just you and me."

One more step backward and Tamara could reach the switch, but she was afraid to take her eyes off Skip for an instant. Would he react if she made a sudden move?

TWELVE

A sudden knock at the door startled Tamara, and Skip reacted swiftly, catching her against him and turning her to face the door. He held the cutting blade next to her bare throat.

Tamara had never been so frightened in her life. The pounding of her heart was nearly suffocating. She could feel the heat of Skip's body engulfing her. He had her trapped against his chest with one arm fastened around her torso, the cold steel of the knife handle pressing at her throat and his hot breath at her ear.

The pounding at the door increased. "Miss Bennington, this is Lieutenant Carlile," the newcomer identified himself. "I need to talk to you."

"Get rid of him," Skip hissed.

"How can I?" Tamara hissed back. "He's not going away, no matter what I say."

Carlile began pounding harder and calling Tamara's name. When there was no response, he warned that he was going to shoot the lock off the door.

Skip pressed the handle of the blade harder against her neck. "Open the door and he can watch while I slice your beautiful throat."

"I'm coming," she managed to yell at Carlile. Skip eased her closer to the door so that she could release the lock. Then he dragged her backward a few steps as the door swung open.

Carlile froze as he took in the situation.

Skip pulled Tamara a few short steps backward. "Get inside and close the door," he commanded the lieutenant. "Where's Masters and the security people?"

"Waiting for me to bring Tamara downstairs," Carlile said.

"Why didn't Masters come after her?"

Skip was getting really nervous. Tamara felt the heightened tension and his mounting frustration. She tried to calm her own breathing. Rane was near. She could feel it.

"He insisted on driving." Carlile answered. "He wanted to drive her to a safe house."

Then the lieutenant amazed Tamara by launching into a description of the charges he intended to file against Skip.

"You'd be wise to release Miss Bennington. You're already in serious trouble with the law. We've got evidence that it was your car that tried to run her down in the parking lot. We have an eyewitness to your aborted abduction of Katie. You'll be slapped with attempted murder, kidnapping, and resisting arrest if you don't cooperate now," Carlile droned on.

Tamara thought he must be crazy. His words just inflamed Skip, making him tighten his hold on her. She was getting a stiff neck from trying to avoid the edge of the cutting blade.

The next instant she heard a thud and felt Skip's body go rigid. The blade was jerked from her neck and Carlile was reaching for her as Skip's body slipped to the floor.

Rane stood over the man he'd knocked unconscious. He'd been forced to use Skip's method of slipping in the bedroom window to approach from behind and unarm Tamara's assailant. He pried the cutting blade from Skip's hand, his own hand trembling now that she was safe. He broke out in a cold sweat as he thought of what could have happened.

Tamara couldn't believe the weaknesses of her knees. She wanted to go to Rane, but her legs refused to support her and she gratefully accepted Carlile's assistance. She realized now that he'd been talking to distract Skip while Rane moved close enough to help.

"Are you all right?" There was a slight quaver in Rane's voice as he tossed aside the blade and reached for Tamara.

She went into his arms and clung to him. "I'm fine."

She pressed her face against his chest and drew strength from the solid width of his body. He wrapped her tightly in his arms and buried his face in her hair, breathing in the familiar scent of her and thanking God that she hadn't been hurt.

Skip was handcuffed while he was still unconscious. The police lieutenant called for back-up officers and assisted Tony as he recovered from his drugged state. Rane pulled Tamara further into the living room as Skip began to stir and people started crowding into her apartment.

"What took you so long?" She finally lifted her head from the comfort of his chest and flashed bright eyes at him.

"I was back in less than an hour, just like I promised," he teased lightly, relieved by her return of spirit.

Tamara released her death grip on his midsection. "Well it seemed like the longest hour I've ever waited."

Rane gave her a wicked grin, but his eyes were serious. "I was at the police station when Carlile got a call about someone coming through your window." He never wanted to experience that kind of gripping fear again. "We got here as fast as we could."

"Rane did insist on driving," Carlile put in. "We made record time."

Skip was regaining consciousness and swore violently as he was pulled to his feet by police officers. He made an ineffective lunge toward Tamara.

"Read him his rights and get him out of here," Carlile ordered.

Rane pressed the palms of his hands over Tamara's ears to block out the sound of Skip's ravings. She gave him a smile of thanks and hugged him again.

Tony came to Rane, looking so dejected that Tamara had to hide a smile.

"I'm sorry, boss. I never even saw the guy. I was just sittin' there and the lights went out."

"Don't worry about it, Tony. No harm was done. If you feel up to it, you can head back out to the Bennington ranch and tell them Reardon's been arrested and jailed."

"Sure thing, boss. I'll be fine," said the big man. He turned to Tamara. "I hope you weren't scared too bad, Mrs. Masters, and I'm sure glad you're all right."

"Thank you, Tony, and thanks for helping us. Will you please tell my family that everything is fine and that I'll call them first thing in the morning?"

"Sure thing, Mrs. Masters," he agreed on his way out. "Good night, boss."

Tamara felt a thrill at the appellation and grinned at Rane. "Should I call you boss, too?"

Rane returned her smile. "You can call me anything you want, Mrs. Masters," he whispered for her ears only. Their intimate exchange was interrupted by Lieutenant Carlile.

"The bedroom window will have to be replaced tomorrow. I locked it again and put a night stick between the broken section and the lock. I'll have a patrolman keep a watch over the place tonight, but you shouldn't have anything to worry about."

Rane reached out a hand and shook Carlile's. Then he and Tamara walked to the door with the lieutenant.

"Thanks for all your help," Rane told him with Tamara echoing the thought. "We'll come to the station tomorrow and take care of legal matters."

"Thank you," replied Carlile. "I'm just sorry we didn't have Reardon in custody before you returned from your honeymoon," he added, tongue in cheek.

Tamara wondered at the strange exchange of glances between the two men, but Rane's only response was to close the door in Carlile's face.

"What was that all about?" she asked him when they were alone.

Rane headed toward Katie's bedroom. "Carlile knows we didn't elope."

Tamara followed him, knowing he wanted to check the window himself. "How does he know that?"

"He was with Harold and me when we planned your abduction," Rane admitted, testing Carlile's makeshift safeguard on the window. He was satisfied that nobody could unlock the window with the stick behind the latch.

Tamara saw the slice of glass Skip had removed from the window and shivered. She was glad he hadn't gotten the chance to use the razor-sharp blade on her.

"Didn't Carlile mention that what you had planned was totally illegal?" she asked him.

"Yes, as a matter-of-fact, he did," Rane replied, turning his full attention on her.

Tamara had to smile, but she put her hands on her hips in a token protest. "Then why did you proceed with a plan that could have landed you in jail?"

Rane leaned against one of the canopy supports of Katie's bed and crossed his arms over his chest. He slowly surveyed Tamara from the top of her head to her bare toes, thinking how incredibly beautiful and desirable she was.

"Maybe I think you're worth any risk," he finally replied.

Tamara looked into his eyes and felt her heart melting. No man had ever looked at her with such a disturbing mixture of love, adoration, and desire.

"Do you still think I'm adorable?" she managed in a soft, husky whisper.

Rane moved and her heart began to pound in frantic excitement. When he cupped her face in his hands, she felt like she might explode with happiness.

"I adore you," he confessed as he pressed a lingering kiss on her lips.

His tender words filled Tamara with a longing she associated solely with him. She shifted closer and the satin of her pajamas swished seductively in the quiet of the room.

"I missed you," she declared as she slipped her arms about his waist and tilted her head back to allow his lips unlimited access to her face.

He kissed her eyes, first one and then the other. He kissed one smooth cheek, her nose and the other cheek. Then his mouth delved beneath the silky curtain of her hair and sought the creamy skin of her neck.

Tamara quivered in his arms as he used his lips and tongue to caress the flesh Skip had touched with the cutting blade. She felt him shudder and knew he was having a delayed reaction to the danger she'd faced.

"I'm sorry," he murmured as his arms enfolded her.

"Sorry for rescuing me again?" she tried to tease, but her voice sounded weak and husky.

"Sorry for leaving you for even one minute."

It was hard to argue while Rane plied the sensitive curve of her neck with warm kisses. "You did everything humanly possible to protect me."

"Speaking of protection," he started, lifting his head to gaze directly into her eyes. "I collected a few things at my apartment to insure your protection. Providing you invite me to spend the night, that is."

Tamara was so close to him that she could feel his heart slamming against his chest. Hers was beating a matching rhythm. "Would you like to spend the night?"

"There's nowhere in the world I'd rather be than with you," he supplied softly.

The yearning in his tone and eyes stole Tamara's breath and made her pulse drum in her ears. She couldn't find words to express how much she wanted him, but she conveyed her wishes.

"Everyone thinks we're married. Tony even called me Mrs. Masters. Three times. So did you. Doesn't that mean you have to carry me over a threshold or something?"

Rane slid one hand down her spine to her hips and then swept her into his arms, drawing her close to his chest. Tamara's arms slipped around his neck and her eyes locked with his.

"Where we goin', big boy?" she asked breathily.

"To the threshold of your bedroom," he told her, eyes blazing.

"Does that mean you're going to spend the night?" she asked while nibbling at his lips with tiny little love bites.

"If you want me to," he countered in a low, rasping tone that expressed the violent effect she was having on him.

Rane had to stop in the living room to kiss her. He captured her marauding lips with his own and kissed her greedily, passionately, thoroughly. Tamara plunged her fingers through his hair and tugged him closer. She returned his kisses with a fervor that quickly ignited uncontrollable desire.

"Dear God, Tamara, you make me weak," Rane moaned against her mouth.

"Better take me to bed, then," she urged seductively.

Rane carried her to her own bedroom, but didn't lay her on the bed. Instead, he stood her on her feet in front of him and fought to dampen his raging desire. He was too hot, too hungry, and too close to losing control.

"We'd better slow down," he warned in a raw tone.

Tamara shook her head negatively, causing a wealth of luxurious curls to dance over her bare shoulders. Her fingers reached out to slowly unbutton his shirt and her eyes met his in undisguised need.

When she parted the front of his shirt and slipped her hands inside the fabric, Rane's hands came up to halt her erotic exploration, but he ended up pressing her fingers closer to his fevered flesh. She played with the curling mass of hair on his chest and then found the tight male nipples hidden beneath the hair. Her light, teasing touch brought forth a rumbling groan from Rane.

"Enough!" he rasped, dragging her hands from his body and planting hot kisses on her palms.

Tamara argued against any restraints. "I want to touch."

Rane closed his eyes and battled for control. "I want it, too, sweetheart, but I want it slow and easy. I want to love you all night long, so you'll have to cooperate."

"Pretty bossy, aren't you?" she teased, feeling a burst of pleasure at his words. She withdrew her hands from his and placed them at her sides, standing perfectly still before him.

"Have it your way, then," she invited provocatively.

A slow, sexy grin spread across Rane's features. "You're my kind of woman, Tammy Jo," he proclaimed, lifting his hands to gently massage her bare shoulders. The heat of his gaze made Tamara's breasts ache with need and her nipples blossom against their satin confinement.

He loved the feel of her skin and stroked the soft flesh of her arms before dropping his thumbs to the nipples that were begging for attention. Tamara's low moan of pleasure caused fire to shoot through his body.

Her knees threatened to buckle, but Rane's strong hands supported her. "Promise me something," he pleaded gruffly, staring into the passion clouded depths of her eyes. "Promise you'll tell me if I do anything that hurts you or scares you."

"Oh, Rane!" she cried. "I know you're not going to do anything that I won't love, but you may drive me crazy with your restraint!"

Rane grinned sexily, wickedly. "Think so?" he taunted, delighted by her impatience. He peeled the satin from her breasts and clamped his hands about her waist, drawing her closer and lifting her slightly so that he could bury his face in the lush softness. He felt her whole body tighten in anticipation and his blood ran hot.

Tamara clutched at his head and thought she would die with longing. Then she tugged at Rane's hair to guide his attention to the turgid, aching peaks of her breasts.

His mouth closed over a nipple and he suckled greedily. Tamara groaned and her fingers clinched in his hair. When he shifted his attention to the other nipple, she emitted a low, tortured moan.

"Do you know what it does to me when I feel the evidence of your desire and hear your sweet moans?" Rane asked hoarsely.

"Tell me," she encouraged.

His mouth captured hers with a ravishing hunger, his arms enveloping her and his whole body transmitting his need. "You make me so hot I feel like I'll burn up before I get close enough to you."

One of her hands slid to his waist and then lower

where she felt the straining evidence of his arousal. "I know exactly what you mean," she whispered. "I get all hot and trembly when I feel how much you want me."

The groan she brought forth from Rane caused a tremor to pass through her body. There was no doubting that she had the power to inflame this big man and the idea made her feel sexy, exciting, and desirable. She wanted to test that power, but Rane quickly put a stop to her tentative caresses.

"Not this time, sweetheart," he declared in a low moan. "This time I want you with me all the way."

Tamara wrapped her arms around his neck and her mouth sought his in fervent demand for more kisses. Her tongue shot into his mouth and challenged his to a heated duel while her body began to writhe against his in an ancient rhythm of mating.

Her breasts were crushed against his naked chest and her hips strained towards the hardness of his loins. She couldn't seem to get close enough to him.

Rane savored the kisses and her seductive aggression. His hands convulsively clutched at her hips and then impatiently slid the satin off her body. She was completely naked beneath the pajamas and his big hands kneaded the baby-soft flesh of her hips while pulling her more tightly into the cradle of his thighs.

Without lifting his mouth from the savage sweetness of hers, Rane lifted Tamara in his arms and carried her the few feet to her bed. He placed her gently on the sheets, easing her slowly backward until she was prone. Then he drew slightly away to savor her beauty.

Her eyes locked with his, shining with slumberous desire and complete trust. Desire clutched at his insides with gripping savagery, but he wanted to touch her, explore her softness, excite her to a fever pitch of arousal.

He started with her feet; massaging, stroking, kissing. Then he investigated every bend and curve of her legs. He caressed and kissed her thighs, then her stomach until he felt her quivering with need.

Tamara arched her hips and growled with impatience. She reached for his head and begged him to hurry his sensuous explorations. When his mouth finally made its way back up to her breasts, she emitted a low, throaty moan.

"Enough!" she insisted huskily. "I can't stand any more!"

Rane laughed with sheer pleasure. He was madly in love with this passionate woman and he couldn't wait to show her just how much pleasure she could withstand. He wanted to make love to her for hours, but not this time.

Rane shrugged out of his shirt and Tamara's hands reached for his belt buckle. "I think I can manage," he teased gruffly. "Any assistance from you will cause serious delays."

"Hurry, then," she insisted, her eyes adoring. She watched him strip and the adoration quickly turned to hot excitement. Her arms lured him back to bed and his body slid over her trembling form. Their breathing quickly became tortured and they rubbed against one another with primitive abandon.

Their mouths locked, their tongues stroking each other wildly, while they strained to get closer. One of Rane's muscular thighs slid between Tamara's and her legs clenched around it, her muscles gripping and demanding.

Rane's moan was low and deep as he dragged his

mouth from hers and renewed his suckling attack on her nipples. When she finally cried out and begged him to come to her, he lost control. He barely managed to protect her before joining their bodies in the most elemental fashion.

Tamara gasped and stiffened when she felt the unbelievable fullness of his possession. Rane went still until her body accepted his. When she wrapped her legs around his thighs and arched towards him, all thought of caution was lost.

He wanted to make her totally his; his woman, his only love. He wanted her to need him as desperately as he needed her. His big body moved with a strong, sure rhythm that he prayed would please Tamara.

She was lost in a mindless world of tumultuous sensations. Rane had made her aware of her own sensuality and the accompanying passion, but nothing could have prepared her for the feel of their bodies locked in love. The tension spiraling in her stole her breath and she clung to Rane with every ounce of strength she could muster.

Tamara's every nerve ending was stretched to the limit of endurance. Suddenly, she was at a pinnacle and still grasping. Rane's forceful movements brought a swift release that sent more shock waves radiating throughout her body.

His powerful body tensed as he felt Tamara's body convulse with tremors of release and heard her cries of pleasure. She seemed to tighten around him, driving him to the same savage satisfaction.

He collapsed onto her softness and Tamara's arms hugged him in a fiercely possessive grip. They battled for breath, but she refused to let him shift his weight.

Together, they slowly came down from their natural high.

Neither of them had slept well the night before, so exhaustion and satisfaction soon took its toll. They slept deeply, wrapped in one another's arms.

Near dawn the next morning, Tamara awakened to the incredibly delicious feeling of warm lips on her neck and warm hands massaging her hips and thighs. She was smiling before she even opened her eyes.

"Good morning," Rane murmured as he felt her wakening. She turned into his arms and curled her body to fit the curve of his.

"Morning," she mumbled as her lips sought the strong line of his throat. She sucked his skin gently and felt him quiver in response to the tiny action.

Rane pulled her tightly against his body and groaned with pleasure at the warm, responsive way she molded herself to him. "I love you," he proclaimed gruffly. His love was so intense that it actually caused him pain.

"I love you, too," Tamara insisted, her voice still husky from sleep.

Rane pulled her on top of him and used both of his hands to massage the length of her spine, his hands growing more insistent as she rocked her hips against his fully-aroused body.

Tamara continued to spread biting little kisses over his face and neck. She sunk her fingers into the thickness of his hair and concentrated on showering him with kisses. She was totally absorbed in her adoration.

Then one of Rane's big hands slid between their bodies and stroked her intimately, shattering her concentration and drawing a deep-throated moan from her.

"Make love to me," he whispered roughly, lifting her and then slowly lowering her to join their bodies.

The air seemed to desert Tamara's lungs and she moaned with pleasure, looking at him with eyes filled with wonder. Would it always be this way? Would she always feel such a wild, pulsing thrill when he became a part of her?

Rane's heart pounded blood through his veins with escalating intensity until he thought he wouldn't survive the raw pleasure. Tamara's awed expression made him feel every inch a man. He pulled her tightly to him, and for the next few minutes, insured that she felt like a much-loved, well-satisfied woman.

Later, he pulled a sheet over their cooling bodies, but didn't allow Tamara to shift far from him. She dozed, but he continued to stroke her smooth flesh and consider the devastating impact she'd made on his heart.

He was hopelessly in love. It was a shocking revelation at this stage in his life. He knew she loved him, too, but he had to find a way to convince her to marry him. She had serious reservations about love and marriage, yet he had to prove to her that she could trust what they felt for one another. He just didn't know how to go about proving love.

Tamara's lashes fluttered open and her sleep-clouded eyes locked with his. She felt a melting warmth as she glimpsed the depth of his love. Her heart ached. Her brain told her it was too good to be true, too good to last, yet her heart cried out a matching need. She desperately wanted Rane's love, but that desperation brought fear and wariness.

"Don't," Rane commanded gruffly, stroking her cheek with a gentle finger. "Don't let the insecurities come between us."

Tamara closed her eyes, uncomfortable with his ability to analyze her thoughts and feelings.

She was quiet for a long time, but Rane knew she wasn't sleeping. She was trying to barricade her emotions behind a wall of caution and reserve.

"Come and live with me at the ranch," he broke the heavy silence by suggesting. "Leave the rat race and be my wife."

Tamara opened her eyes and looked at him. "You know I can't do that."

"Can't or won't?"

"I can't." She'd dreaded this inevitable battle and had hoped to postpone it for a few more days. "You know what the business world is like. I've already been gone a month. If I don't take up the reins of control soon, there will be a lot of speculation and stock prices will fall. I've worked too hard to sit back and let it all self-destruct. There's no one to take my place. Harold's retired, he feels like he's too old, and Katie's too young."

Her arguments fell on deaf ears. Rane wanted her with him, always. He didn't care about anything but having her by his side. "You can delegate corporate responsibilities," he declared. "Is the business your only concern?"

"I have other responsibilities," Tamara insisted. "I don't go anywhere without Katie. I've been told that a teenage girl is a burden on newlywed couples, but her upbringing is a responsibility that I don't intend to delegate."

"I'm not Reardon," Rane clipped in annoyance. "I understand how you feel. Katie is welcome to live with us."

Tamara moved to her own side of the bed, pulling

the sheet protectively over her breasts. She knew Rane meant what he said, but he lived alone and had no idea what it would be like.

"Katie plays a trumpet, she's a cheerleader, she loves loud music, and spends hours on the telephone," Tamara felt compelled to inform him. "We wouldn't have much privacy."

Rane clenched his teeth in frustration. "You're making excuses and using Katie as a shield. I said I wanted her and I meant it. I expect her to behave like a normal teenager."

Tamara darted a glance at him. "Do you mean that?"

"I mean it. I want you both to make your home with me."

"But what if it doesn't work?" She felt compelled to consider the drawbacks of his idea. "What if I disrupt all our lives; force my family to make adjustments, restructure the business, and then we can't make it work?"

Rane's expression grew grim. "What if the passion wears off? What if you stop wanting me? What if the love isn't strong enough?" he derided. "I don't want a 'what if' marriage, Tamara. I want a real, lifetime commitment."

"You want me to just give up everything that I've worked for and run away with you," she challenged. "You chose to leave the corporate world, but I haven't. I don't know how to be a ranch wife. I don't even know if I want to try," she admitted. "I think it would be best to make the adjustments gradually. I could spend time at your ranch and you could stay in the city once in a while until we're sure marriage is what we really want."

"Like an illicit love affair?" he snarled, his eyes flashing with resentment. "All the perks, but none of the risks? A little fling that you could end when the going gets rough?"

Tamara paled at his interpretation of her suggestion. "I didn't mean we should sneak around and hide how we feel. All of Texas thinks we're married!"

Rane angrily pulled on his clothes. His shower would have to wait. "And all of Texas will be waiting to see what we do now that we're home."

"So is this really an issue of masculine pride?" Tamara lashed, her temper rising. "Did you ask me to come home with you because that's the manly thing to do?" she demanded tartly.

"Pride has something to do with it," Rane snapped. "So does love, possessiveness, and protective instincts. I want a full-time mate, not a part-time playmate!"

Tamara gasped at the belittling of what they shared. She'd never suggested that they be playmates or that they indulge in a part-time love affair. She just couldn't see why they had to burn all their bridges behind them.

"Have I shocked you?" Rane's question was launched as he retrieved his wallet from the bedside stand. He stretched his long length across the bed and cupped Tamara's face in one big hand. His eyes shone with a depth of emotion that frightened her and his words seared her soul.

"I love you more than I thought it was possible to love a woman. I want you with me every day when I wake up, when I go to bed, and anytime in between when it's humanly possible.

"This last month with you spoiled me," he continued, his voice gruff with emotion. "I've learned that I can't accept half measures where you're concerned. I want everything you have to give: your love, your trust, your loyalty, and a promise of a lifetime together. Anything short of that will never be enough!''

Tamara trembled in the face of such a deep, overwhelming, all-consuming commitment. ''I don't know if I have that much courage,'' she admitted hoarsely.

Rane's eyes mirrored his pain. ''You don't know if you love me nearly as much as I love you,'' he supplied. ''You're afraid to trust me. That's the bottom line.''

Tamara started to argue, but he swiftly put distance between them and cut off any further discussion. Then his attitude became cool, efficient, and indifferent.

''I promised Carlile we'd come to the police station this morning. As soon as I'm sure you'll be safe, I need to get my men back to the ranch. There's only a skeleton crew at home and they can't work that way for much longer.''

Rane turned from her, adding, ''I'll call someone to replace Katie's bedroom window and wait in the living room until you're dressed.'' The door closed quietly behind him.

_____ THIRTEEN _____

By late that afternoon Rane was gone. Tamara had chosen to stay in the city and he had gone to his ranch. He'd taken care of everything, just as he'd promised, and Tamara found herself wandering aimlessly around her apartment. She knew she should go to Harold's ranch, but she wasn't ready to face all the questions.

Rane's attitude had remained polite for the whole day and his cool indifference had cut her heart to pieces. She couldn't bear it. She couldn't stand to have him reject her in any fashion, even though it was her fault he'd been so distant.

He loved her. She knew it. So why had his attitude hurt so much? Why had his cool good-bye kiss made her want to scream and beg and weep?

It was early evening when Tamara called her family and told them she wouldn't be out until the next morning. Her emotions were too chaotic to face anyone. She locked her doors, turned out the lights, and headed for the bedroom.

That was her mistake. Everything in the room reminded her of the night she'd spent with Rane. Tamara fell to the bed and pulled the sheets and blankets around her fully-clothed body. They still carried Rane's scent and her control was completely shattered. Tears began to roll down her cheeks and she made no attempt to stop them.

She hadn't wept over anything or anybody since she'd buried her mother. When she'd carried Katie down that mountain, the tears had poured from her eyes, soaking her face until the freezing temperature had frozen them into a sheet of ice.

The frozen mask had stayed intact until now. She'd been hiding behind it for a long time. Now the heat of her tears was melting her defenses and making her vulnerable again. As she sobbed, she bared her rawest emotions for self-analysis. It hurt, but she had to admit to herself that she'd been wrong about so many things.

When the weeping gradually slowed to a stop, Tamara felt cleansed. Ridding herself of years of pent-up anger, frustration, and pain had a cathartic effect.

Thanks to Rane's patience and love, she was finally able to understand the depth of love her parents had shared. She no longer condemned them for leaving her. She no longer felt the need to hide from her past, and putting the two parts of her life back together made her whole again.

As a whole person, she was free to love Rane. She could go to him without emotional baggage and offer him her heart without condition.

Making the decision lightened her heart even more. Tamara spent the rest of the night thinking, planning, and dreaming about marriage to the man she loved.

Putting her plans into effect wasn't quite so easy.

She wanted to go to Rane with a clear conscious, so she had to wait until she'd discussed her plans with her family and staff. Lots of people would be making adjustments to accommodate her new schedule, and she wanted to take care of business first.

With the exception of her family, she allowed everyone to go on believing that she was married, and that the new working arrangements would allow her more time with Rane. It was mostly the truth.

Tamara prayed every day of the long week they were parted. She prayed that he would call. When he didn't, she prayed that he hadn't changed his mind about wanting her. She prayed, and planned, and worked feverishly to free herself for another short vacation. This time she was hoping for a real honeymoon.

A little over a week after Rane left the city, Tamara and Katie were on their way to his ranch. Katie had been wildly excited about spending some time at Rane's and Tamara hoped they wouldn't be turned away once they arrived.

She hadn't heard a word from him since the day they'd argued and he didn't know she was coming. The thought of seeing him within minutes was making her insane with anticipation and apprehension. The "what ifs" had plagued her daily since she'd decided that nothing in her life was worth more than what she shared with Rane.

"Tammy, there it is!" Katie cried, pointing toward the impressive gateway to the "Flying Masters" ranch. Katie had been navigating according to Harold's directions and Tamara had driven where she was directed. She was glad they'd reached their destination, but she grew more tense with each minute.

"Do you think Rane will be at home?" Katie asked, trying to take in everything at a glance.

"I hope so," was Tamara's reply. They'd traveled northeast of San Antonio and were finding more fertile grazing land. The summer weather had been kind to Texans by supplying enough rainfall to keep rivers running with water. Rane's land looked rich with green grass and gigantic shade trees.

Cattle grazed on either side of the driveway and the herds looked enormous to them. Neither of them had much experience on a working ranch. Since they'd lived in Texas they'd become full-fledged city girls.

"You're not ready to change your mind and go back to San Antone, are you?" Tamara asked her sister.

"No way!" exclaimed Katie with the same enthusiasm she'd expressed since the subject of living with Rane had been introduced. She'd spent considerable time lecturing Tamara about love, romance, and happily-ever-afters.

They both caught their breath when Rane's house finally came into view. It was big and sprawling and the most inviting place Tamara had ever seen. The huge, three-storied frame didn't conform to any classical lines of architecture and couldn't be described as modern, but it had aesthetic appeal that was unique.

It had character and Tamara loved it on sight. She brought the car to a halt in front of the veranda that seemed to circle the entire building, then dragged her attention back to her sister. "Rane obviously wasn't kidding when he said he had plenty of space," she said.

"I guess not," Katie replied, shifting her gaze to Tamara. "Let's just hope he wasn't kidding about wanting us."

Tamara's heart leapt at the thought, but she managed to laugh at Katie's uncharacteristic uncertainty. Katie was nervous, but not nearly as nervous as she.

Slipping her feet back into strappy sandals, she gave Katie a reassuring grin. "There's only one way to find out," she teased, opening her door and coming quickly around to the passenger side. She grasped Katie's hand and they both giggled as they stepped up to the veranda and approached the front door.

The door was already open and a small dog began to bark furiously behind the screen door. The feisty Pekingese was hushed by a tall, dark-haired woman. As soon as her deep brown eyes took in the sight of the two sisters, she swung open the door and greeted them warmly.

"You have to be Tamara and Katie," she exclaimed, her tone surprised and pleased. "Rane told me the two of you were the most beautiful women in Texas, but I admit I was a little skeptical. I sincerely apologize," she teased, giving them both an unexpected, but welcomed hug.

"I'm his mother, by the way, Eleanor Hudson," she added with a grin. "I've been staying with him while some remodeling is being done at my house. He didn't even tell me you were coming."

"He doesn't know," supplied Katie, making a face that proclaimed her disapproval. "I told Tamara we should call, but she insisted on surprising him."

Eleanor laughed. "I can guarantee he'll be surprised. He's been as restless as a stallion since he came home from his vacation."

Tamara couldn't prevent the blush that heated her cheeks. She had no idea how Rane had explained their unusual relationship to his mother.

"Is he home?" she asked, smoothing a wrinkle from her buttercup yellow sun dress. Her hair was a loose mass of curls falling on bare shoulders and she brushed it nervously from her face while praying that Rane was close.

"He's out back working with the horses. I'll send somebody to find him while I get the two of you something cool to drink."

"If you don't mind," Tamara reached out and halted the other woman's movement toward the door. Her eyes begged for understanding. "I'd like to find him myself. I'm sure Katie would love something to drink, but I want to see Rane first."

Eleanor's shrewd eyes acknowledged understanding without taking offense. She smiled reassuringly.

"If you go around the side of the house, you'll see the barn and surrounding corrals. Rane's probably working in the one that's left of the barn doors."

"Thanks," Tamara said, smiling warmly. Then she glanced at her sister. She hated to just desert her.

Eleanor reached for one of Katie's hands. "Don't worry about Katie. I'm sure we'll find plenty of things to talk about. It's been a while since I had a teenager around and I need to catch up on the latest fads."

"Go on," Katie insisted. "Go kiss and make up."

Tamara's blush deepened and she shook her head in resignation at her sister's impudence. "Mind your manners," she scolded lightly. "I won't be long." She turned away while Katie told Eleanor that she didn't get enough respect.

The smile froze on her face as she rounded the veranda and headed across the yard toward the barn. The "what ifs" were plaguing her again, shattering her self-confidence, and making her nerves raw. Her stomach churned and her pulse beat frantically. She couldn't bear the thought that Rane might have changed his mind about wanting her.

As she neared the corral at the left of the barn, she saw several men watching the activity within the fenced area. When she was close enough to lean against the fence, she saw what was holding their attention. Rane was mounted on a giant, angry beast that was determined to unseat him in a violent fashion. The horse reared, twisted, and kicked.

Tamara's heart rose to her throat and fear nearly choked her as she watched Rane soar over the horse's head and hit the ground with a thud. A silent scream of horror was trapped in her chest until a ranch hand restrained the horse.

Rane came to his feet with a graceful ease that belied any injury, but his curses filled the air as he gave vent to the horse's contrariness.

Tamara felt giddy with relief as she watched him angrily brush the dust from his clothes, still swearing. He was so big and strong and precious to her. Her heart swelled with pride as laughter bubbled inside of her.

"Hey, Masters," she called to him, her feminine voice quieting all other conversation. "Is that how you developed a penchant for flying?"

If Tamara lived to be two hundred years old, she'd never forget the look on Rane's face as his eyes fastened on her. There was no time to guard his reaction to her presence and the aching intensity of his love and longing was clearly displayed on his rugged features.

His dark eyes lit with joy and his mouth curved in a smile so bold that it made her heart pound a heavy cadence in her chest. When he began to walk toward her, every nerve and muscle in her body constricted with anticipation and wild elation.

Rane kept dusting the dirt from his clothes as he approached Tamara, but his eyes never left her for an instant. She was so beautiful that she stole his breath.

The sun enhanced the golden highlights in her hair and the satin sheen of her bare shoulders. The short, strapless dress she was wearing displayed her lovely figure and slim legs, making him ache to touch her.

He mentally warned himself that she might not be here to stay, yet he couldn't contain his pleasure at seeing her again. He'd missed her badly and had decided he wanted her on any terms, but he was glad she'd come to him.

"Hi," he greeted her as he stopped on the opposite side of the fence. He didn't reach out to touch her, but his eyes devoured her.

"Hi, yourself," Tamara returned, her heart in her eyes.

"Come with me," Rane instructed huskily as he vaulted the fence and reached for her hand. He ignored the teasing jeers of his men and led Tamara toward the barn.

A rush of heat suffused her body and her fingers clung tightly to his as she followed him through the open barn door. While her eyes adjusted to the dim lighting, Rane released her hand and moved toward an old-fashioned water basin.

He swiftly tugged off his shirt and filled the sink from a hand pump. When the water was flowing freely, he sluiced it over his head, chest, and arms.

Tamara smiled when she realized that he wasn't going to welcome her properly until he was clean. She was aching to be in his arms, but she enjoyed watching his impromptu bath. His muscles rippled and water trickled through the curling hair on his chest. His every movement emphasized his strength and her eyes feasted on him. Her frantic heartbeat could not be calmed.

When Rane had towel dried, he ran combing fingers through his thick hair and turned his full attention on Tamara. His eyes shimmered with love, longing, and a bit of wicked delight.

"Now, I'd like a proper hello," he commanded softly.

Tamara was in his arms in an instant, her own arms locking about his neck as she pressed herself as close to him as possible. She felt the iron-hard strength of his hands pulling her tightly against him and she moaned her delight at being so close.

Her mouth met his in an ardent proclamation of love. She welcomed the thrusting invasion of his tongue with an urgency that left them both shaken. Their breathing quickly grew ragged as they fought to lessen the agony of being parted for so long.

"I missed you so much," Tamara murmured against his mouth when their lips finally parted for air.

"I missed you more," he argued huskily, capturing her mouth for another long, deep kiss. She tasted so sweet and he'd been starving. He held her tighter and kissed her until they had no air left to breathe.

The next time their lips parted, he ran his over every beloved feature of her face and then buried his nose in the intoxicating sweetness of her hair. He inhaled deeply and moaned his pleasure at the familiar scent of her.

Tamara kissed the firm outline of his jaw and then pressed kisses over his throat and neck. She nuzzled her face against the curve of his shoulder and heaved a contented sigh.

"Ever make love in a barn?" Rane queried gruffly. His hands dropped to her hips and he pulled her into the hardened cradle of his thighs, making her fully aware of his urgent need for her.

"No," Tamara replied breathlessly. The eyes that met his were shining with happiness. "But if I experiment now, Katie and your mother will probably send out a search party."

"Katie's here?" Rane asked in surprise, his eyes suddenly searching the depths of hers.

Tamara pulled back slightly and frowned. "You said she was welcome."

"Of course, she's welcome," he insisted, realizing that his reaction had alarmed her. "I wanted you to bring her out, but I guess I didn't expect it to happen."

"I never suggested that I didn't want you and Katie to get to know each other better."

"But you strongly suggested that I didn't know how to cope with a teenager," he reminded, rocking her gently in his arms. "And you were adamant about not burdening me with her presence."

Tamara smiled and kneaded the firm flesh covering his ribs. "You might still change your mind, but I consider my duty done by warning you."

Rane grinned and stole another kiss. He wanted so much more, but it was broad daylight and his ranch was crawling with employees. He moaned as Tamara's tongue teased the length of his and knew he'd better cool his ardor for a while.

"Maybe we should go up to the house," he suggested with little enthusiasm.

Tamara laughed softly. "I suppose you're right," she agreed, taking another kiss.

Rane finally managed to set her away from him. Tamara worked at regulating her breathing while Rane slid his arms back into his shirt.

They blinked in the sunlight as they left the barn and then smiled brilliantly at one another as they walked toward the house.

"You have a gorgeous home," she complimented. "I haven't been inside, but the whole place has character."

Rane laughed and his tone was filled with pride. "That's exactly what I thought when I bought it." He was pleased that she liked it. He still didn't know what had prompted her visit or if he could tempt her to stay, but he needed every edge he could use.

Rounding the side of the house, Rane caught sight of the station wagon Tamara had driven. "Why don't I think that's your usual mode of transportation?"

"It's not, but I couldn't fit all our things in my little car." She held her breath while he digested that piece of information. His expression didn't alter.

Rane stepped up on the veranda and drew Tamara up to face him. His eyes were locked with hers as he carefully phrased the next question. "Are you planning to stay a while?"

"We'd like to stay a couple of days," she explained.

"Just a couple of days? This is a short visit, then?" he concluded, his facial features stiffening. He didn't like it, but he'd already decided that he would take whatever time Tamara felt capable of giving.

Tamara's mouth went dry and she moistened her lips while she formulated a response. Her eyes searched his, and she drew on all her reserves of courage. Then she reached into the pocket of her dress and pulled out a velvet ring box, holding it up for Rane to see.

Flipping open the lid, Tamara displayed a pair of matching wedding bands; beautiful, glistening, circles of gold.

Rane didn't move a muscle or bat an eye. He was too afraid that he was reading more into the gesture than she intended. He waited, barely daring to breathe, until she explained.

Tamara was so tense that she could barely get the words she wanted to say past her tight throat. She'd rehearsed them for a week, but her voice was still soft and shaky.

"I love you, Rane Masters, and I want to marry you and spend the rest of my life with you. I was a fool for ever letting you leave my side, and I prayed that you still wanted me. I thought if I bought the rings and moved in, it would be more difficult to reject my proposal."

"What about your work? Won't you miss it? What about the future of the business? Do you really think you can walk away from your career?" Rane wanted to reach for her and promise her anything. He wanted it so desperately that he was trembling, yet he needed to be certain that she didn't harbor any fears of marriage.

"I'm not planning to retire or end my career," she answered, her eyes begging him to understand.

"Maybe you'd better explain," he drawled softly.

Tamara nervously replied. "I've discussed the situation with Harold, my assistants, and the board of directors," she began, the ring box quivering slightly in her fingers. "They agree that it's not necessary for me to be at the office every day. Uncle Harold says he's bored with retirement and would like to work part-time. I have dependable people working for me and I can delegate authority, while continuing to make the major decisions. Most of my work can be accomplished by phone or with a couple of days a week at the office.''

She was breathless after her little speech, but she'd noticed that Rane was visibly relaxing. It encouraged her to move close to him again and plant her hands on his broad chest, pressing the ring box between them. All the longing in her heart was in her eyes as she explained how she'd included him in her plans.

''Uncle Harold was kind enough to remind me that the man I love is an excellent pilot with aircraft at his disposal. We hoped he wouldn't mind flying me to the office once or twice a week.''

Rane's eyes were turbulent with emotion, but he didn't immediately respond and Tamara shifted closer. ''Would you mind?'' she pleaded huskily, brushing her lips across his.

''Not if I can have you with me all the rest of the time,'' he conceded hoarsely, his arms enfolding her. He allowed her to play with his mouth for a little while before growing impatient. Then the force of his hungry kiss tipped her head backward and arched her body to fit his own. He adored her mouth with lips and tongue until they were gasping for breath.

''Are you really ready to trust me with your love?'' he asked roughly.

Tamara's response was throaty. ''Yes.'' She answered without qualification. ''I knew within minutes of your leaving me that I couldn't bear life without you. You make me whole.''

Rane groaned and captured her mouth with his, hugging her closer, and trying to show her how much her faith meant to him. Long minutes later, he raised his head and eased his hold on her. Brushing a lock of hair from her cheek, he looked deeply into her eyes, and spoke huskily. "We can work it out. All I needed to know was that you trust me and want a lifetime commitment."

"I do," she swore solemnly, then laughed at her choice of words.

Rane laughed with her, but then his face took on a stern expression. "Why did you wait so damned long to come to me? This has been one of the longest weeks of my life."

"I wanted to take care of business before I came to you. Katie and I hoped we could spend a couple of days here and that you'd return to San Antonio with us next weekend."

"What's happening in San Antonio next weekend?"

"We're getting married, I hope," Tamara told him, her heart in her eyes. "Will you marry me?" she asked him, softly and sincerely.

"Yes . . . yes . . . yes." His reply was interspersed with short, adoring kisses. "Are we having a small ceremony with family and friends?"

"That's the plan being hatched by Katie and Lucinda," Tamara explained, chasing his lips with an equally eager mouth.

"Good women, those Benningtons," Rane murmured. "I don't have to be honorable and not touch you until then, do I?"

Tamara's laughter pealed musically while she shook her head with vigor. "No, sir, you certainly don't."

Rane clutched her close and murmured his love in her ear while hugging her tightly. Their hearts beat together and he kissed her long and hard, then kissed her gently and repeatedly, then kissed her hungrily once more. He just couldn't get enough of her.

Tamara reluctantly eased from his arms when they heard approaching voices. Katie and Eleanor rounded the corner of the porch an instant later.

"We wondered if you got lost," Katie declared, taking in Tamara's disheveled state and shining eyes. "I guess you two kissed and made up," she commented cheekily. "Hi, big brother."

"Hello, princess," Rane countered, giving her a hug. "It's about time you came to see me."

"Sometimes Tamara is *so* slow," Katie insisted, rolling her eyes as she returned his hug.

"I know what you mean," he agreed, flashing her a wicked grin.

Tamara exchanged a knowing smile with Eleanor. "I had an idea that bringing these two together could cause trouble."

"I know what you mean," Eleanor echoed her son's words.

"I'm never any trouble," Rane argued as he slid a possessive arm about Tamara's waist. "Mom, could you show Katie the bedrooms upstairs and let her take her pick. Then have Tony unload their suitcases from the car while I show Tamara around the house."

"No problem," his mother was quick to agree. "I've already given Katie a tour of the downstairs, so we'll go upstairs. When she's settled, I'll get some supper ready."

"Do I really get my choice of rooms?" Katie squealed her delight. She locked arms with Eleanor and they turned to go. "If you help me choose a room and get unpacked, I'll be glad to help fix supper."

"It's a deal," Eleanor said as they headed in the house.

"They're going to be good friends," Rane decided with satisfaction.

"I think you might be right," Tamara teased.

"I've been begging Mom to move in with me for the past five years, but she kept refusing. When I came home from Missouri, we had a long talk and I think she feels comfortable with me for the first time in years. Maybe Katie will be an added incentive to make her change her mind."

"You talked to her about your release from prison?" Tamara asked as they slowly approached the front door.

"Yes, and thanks to some advice from a very knowledgeable lady," he nodded toward her, "we've finally made our peace."

"I'm glad," said Tamara. She halted just outside the door and took his face between her hands. "Because I love you so much and I want you to be the happiest man on this earth."

Rane closed his eyes and blindly gathered her close to his heart. When he reopened his eyes, they were dark and shimmering with emotion. "Your love and faith in me have already made me the happiest man in the world."

"Really?" she breathed in awe.

Rane threw back his head and laughed. His heart swelled with pride and happiness and love that had no end. He lifted Tamara into his arms and opened the door with his foot.

"Welcome to our home, Tamara Jo Bennington, soon-to-be Masters," he proclaimed huskily. "We've got one more threshold to cross."

"I'm ready," she told him as she tightened her hold on his neck and kissed him soundly.

SHARE THE FUN . . .
SHARE YOUR NEW-FOUND TREASURE!!

You don't want to let your new books out of your sight? That's okay. Your friends can get their own. Order below.

No. 29 FOSTER LOVE by Janis Reams Hudson
Morgan comes home to claim his children but Sarah claims his heart.

No. 30 REMEMBER THE NIGHT by Sally Falcon
Joanna throws caution to the wind. Is Nathan fantasy or reality?

No. 31 WINGS OF LOVE by Linda Windsor
Mac & Kelly soar to new heights of ecstasy. Are they ready?

No. 32 SWEET LAND OF LIBERTY by Ellen Kelly
Brock has a secret and Liberty's freedom could be in serious jeopardy!

No. 33 A TOUCH OF LOVE by Patricia Hagan
Kelly seeks peace and quiet and finds paradise in Mike's arms.

No. 34 NO EASY TASK by Chloe Summers
Hunter is wary when Doone delivers a package that will change his life.

No. 35 DIAMOND ON ICE by Lacey Dancer
Diana could melt even the coldest of hearts. Jason hasn't a chance.

No. 36 DADDY'S GIRL by Janice Kaiser
Slade wants more than Andrea is willing to give. Who wins?

No. 37 ROSES by Caitlin Randall
It's an inside job & K.C. helps Brett find more than the thief!

No. 38 HEARTS COLLIDE by Ann Patrick
Matthew finds big trouble and it's spelled P-a-u-l-a.

No. 39 QUINN'S INHERITANCE by Judi Lind
Gabe and Quinn share an inheritance and find an even greater fortune.

No. 40 CATCH A RISING STAR by Laura Phillips
Justin is seeking fame; Beth helps him find something more important.

No. 41 SPIDER'S WEB by Allie Jordan
Silvia's quiet life explodes when Fletcher shows up on her doorstep.

No. 42 TRUE COLORS by Dixie DuBois
Julian helps Nikki find herself again but will she have room for him?

No. 43 DUET by Patricia Collinge
Adam & Marina fit together like two perfect parts of a puzzle!

No. 44 DEADLY COINCIDENCE by Denise Richards
J.D.'s instincts tell him he's not wrong; Laurie's heart says trust him.

No. 45 PERSONAL BEST by Margaret Watson
Nick is a cynic; Tess, an optimist. Where does love fit in?